MY Minotaur HUSBAND

STORIES FROM NEW EDEN

LYONNE RILEY

Introduction

Celeste is one of only a hundred remaining humans on Earth, living on a secured preserve away from the many dangerous monsters out in the world. But some monsters desperately want human companions—and they'll abide by all the strict rules and requirements to get one. Celeste has applications piling up from those who want to court her, but she's afraid of taking the leap... until Theo.

Theo the minotaur is shy, gentle, and kind, and wants nothing more than a human wife to spoil. When Celeste agrees to move in and start a trial marriage, he'll do anything in his power to keep her happy and safe in a world where a human might make a great meal for another monster.

The only problem? Theo is huge in more than one way—and he knows Celeste isn't ready for him yet. It will take trust and time to prepare her as they start to build their new life together, and it might just lead to falling in love.

Content Warnings

- Graphic depictions of sex
- Use of sex toys
- Stretching and stuffing
- Light gore and assault
- Discussion of parental death and abandonment

Chapter One

There are only a hundred of us left, probably fewer now since the last time I counted. We've lost two of the more elderly humans, while many of our number have married off, leaving the rest of us behind.

The best we can hope for on the New Eden preserve is to find a partner and move away, hopefully for good.

Luckily for those who remain, we're a desirable commodity. Monsters send in applications months in advance just to get a chance to meet a human, and even then, our approval isn't guaranteed. My friend Maddie went home with two other monsters for a trial marriage—first an incubus, then a shadow demon—just to test out what their homes were like and what kind of life they would give her. Each time she came back disappointed, until she found Egorr, the big ogre with a heart of gold.

I can't imagine what the sex is like. He's probably eight feet tall and could lift a car without trying. But whenever I get on a Zoom call with Maddie, she seems happy. Egorr's usually in the background, cooking something for them. He dotes on her hand

and foot. That's the promise they make: that we'll have our needs met, and they'll worship us if we give them the chance.

Like Maddie, I don't know what I want yet. Unlike Maddie, I'm not bold enough to meet a monster, not to mention go home with one and try out married life. Then we'll be alone together, and who knows what could happen to me? A monster could flip out on a dime and decide I'm their next meal.

And what if I don't want to stay? What if I have to say "no" and return to the preserve? I can't imagine breaking someone's heart like that—and I don't know if I could stand the disappointment myself.

Besides, living out in the world is risky for a human like me. I'm small and helpless, really, in a river full of piranhas. As much as I long to see the outside world, to experience all the things we can't get at New Eden, it's dangerous to venture out, even with a monster at your side.

So I turn away almost every application I get. On the rare occasion that I have accepted a visit request, we don't mesh at all. Once I sat down with a centaur, but all she wanted to talk about was where she got her nails and hooves done, and her favorite hair conditioner.

I wonder if I'm not cut out for it. Maybe I'm not supposed to get married at all, and I'll just get old and die on the preserve like Julianne did.

It's hard not to feel lonely with both Julianne and Maddie gone now. I tend to the garden we all share, and occasionally someone will join me to pull out weeds, and we'll have a conversation about the weather or the bugs being especially bad this year. Rob is my only close friend on the preserve. It's a cool, quiet day when he shows up after lunch to help me with some transplanting that I've been putting off.

"You've been quiet lately," he says as we pull the seedlings out of their nests in the starter box.

"Nah," I say. "You're just used to Maddie blabbing all the time."

Rob chuckles. "Maybe. She kind of forced you to crawl out of your cave, didn't she?"

I take offense to that. Sure, I'm not the most approachable person, but it's not like I'm a sullen bridge troll.

He's right, though—I do miss her. It feels even less like home without Maddie flitting around and chattering all the time.

"It's less of a *cave* and more of a *den*," I say, digging out a little hole for one of the seedlings. "Really, though, I'm fine. Just life as usual here."

Rob doesn't speak as he continues patting the soil around the base of a plant. Then he turns to me with a serious look on his face.

"Don't you want more than that, Celeste?" Rob asks. "More than just 'life as usual' in the walled garden?"

We each have our own small home, a space to call ours. I've decorated mine with a few houseplants, a reproduction painting or two in chintzy black frames, even a vase. "We have more than we could ever want here," I say. "What do any monsters have that I don't already?"

Rob shrugs. "Companionship. Sex. All the things that people have been sharing with each other since the dawn of time."

I considered marrying Rob once upon a time. Wouldn't it be ideal to extend the human species? But I find that I don't care about the "species." When we're gone, we're gone. Besides, I like Rob as a friend and that's about it.

His voice drops a little. "Don't forget that you'd have safety, too. And freedom. You could leave without being afraid."

The big world outside. New Eden can seem like its own small, tame universe with the convenience store and the parks and the fake little river that divides it in half. It's easy to forget there's more out in the wider world.

Maddie gets to go out to dinner with Egorr. They see movies, walk along the boardwalk, and visit museums—all sorts of things I can't really go do as a lone human, fragile and small, in a world where a stray basilisk might try to swallow me whole.

"I'm not going to marry someone just so I have a body-guard," I say, jamming my spade into the dirt. "That's not fair."

No, when I marry someone, I want it to be for the right reasons. I want it to be for life. Maybe that's too romantic of me, too unrealistic, but I just can't see myself walking down the aisle with someone because I want to go to the movies safely.

"Then marry someone for love." Rob stands up and dusts off his knees. "You can't meet them unless you try, though."

He's right, of course. But there's a lot of risk that comes with trying.

"Just look at a few of the applications, okay?" Rob arches an eyebrow at me. "Maybe you'll find something surprising."

I narrow my eyes. "What about you? All this sage advice from someone who's still here."

Rob shrugs. "I'm dating Rassa. We didn't click immediately, but there's time." Right, the orc woman with a braid down to her butt and a stack of muscles that could pop my head like a blueberry.

I'm surprised. He doesn't really talk about her. "I didn't realize you were still together," I say. "I thought you'd have done a trial marriage by now."

He sits back on his heels. "Taking it slow."

Maybe he's right. Maybe I should at least try. You don't know what could walk in the door until you open it.

"Fine." I finish planting the last seedling, thinking of the stack of applications waiting for me at home. I feel a twinge of anxiety at the idea of meeting any of the monsters who have applied for me, but I could get lucky, like Maddie did with Egorr. "I'll give it a try."

That night I sit down at my little breakfast table to sort through the last batch of applications I got.

Ghoul. Not quite tangible enough for anything fun in bed to happen, and I know if I'm after a life partner, that will definitely be part of the equation.

Next.

Imp. Too mischievous. More likely to ruin the laundry than do it.

Next.

Merman? Hmm. It would be tricky with one of us land-bound and the other ocean-bound, but maybe it could work. Except he says on his application that he likes watching sports, specifically water polo, and that's a huge no-no for me.

Next.

There's a fairy looking for someone to share her tree home, and a reanimated corpse searching for a partner who doesn't mind the smell. I am, of course, neither of those. Heights aren't my strength.

One of the applications makes me pause. He's a minotaur who works in construction, which I know entails long hours and lots of manual labor. It's his answers to the interview questions that draw my attention.

"I want someone to spoil," the application reads. "Someone to go to the movies with me, to go out to dinner with me, to help me make my house a home. She needs to like dogs because I have two of them. I'm a good cook as long as meat isn't involved, and I'm clean. I know how to do my own laundry and I actually like grocery shopping."

I wonder if he's just giving answers he thinks will attract me, or if he's being honest about himself. It sounds like he enjoys venturing out and living life—just what I would want to do if I could go and explore the world. Plus, I've always loved dogs, even though we don't have many of them on the compound.

I want someone to spoil. The moment I read the words, I think I want to be that someone. What if I had a monster I could love and depend on? A companion who would give me a safe home, who could hold me with a soft pair of arms?

Fine. I'm going to take Rob's advice and ask to meet him. Maybe if we click—and this minotaur is telling the truth about himself—I could have that life, too.

I turn in the application at the front desk. "I'd like to make an appointment with Theo," I tell the relationship coordinator. She seems surprised to see me.

"I'll contact him right away," she says, pleased. "I'm sure he'll be happy to hear from you."

Guilt turns my stomach. I'm probably not going to like him, and then I'll be wasting his time. For someone who works construction, that lost time could be a big deal. But the coordinator has taken the application behind the desk already, and it's too late to go back now.

Chapter Two

The meeting with Theo is scheduled for Tuesday, so I have three days to stew over the choice I've made. I research everything about minotaurs in the meantime: how they average seven-and-a-half feet tall, not including the horns. How they came from Greece originally, but now a small population live in most countries around the world. How they typically have mild manners but can sometimes boast a hot temper. I'm not sure what to expect from Theo, and I hope he's not the kind that has a temper.

Rob tries to quell my anxiety. "You haven't even met him yet," he says over lunch in the cafeteria. "Don't judge him before you get to know him."

Of course he's right. I can't write Theo off when I only have a few sentences to go on.

My brain is churning through other questions, too. What if I do like him? What happens then? Go on a few dates, then uproot my life like Maddie did and move in with him to test the waters? I think about the pictures I saw online of minotaurs—

massive creatures with the head of an ox, and fur rolling down their bodies to huge haunches and a short, slender tail.

What if we want to have sex? How does that even work?

There's not a lot online with humans so few and far between, and I have no answers as Tuesday finally rolls around. Theo is meeting me at ten in the morning. He must be taking time off of work to come in. I hope I don't disappoint him.

My heart beats fast and fluttery as I wait in one of the lounges for Theo to arrive. At exactly ten, the opposite door opens, and a wide, towering figure steps inside.

Oh, he's tall. I knew to expect that, but now that I'm faced with his truly gargantuan shape, it takes me by surprise. He has to tilt his head to fit his curved horns through the doorway. He wears a tight-fitting white t-shirt over his huge chest, clearly outlining each of his rounded pectorals and thick, sturdy belly. I can tell there's solid muscle under there, even if it's not as defined, and I know right away he's telling the truth about what he does for work. This isn't a body built in a gym, but by hard labor. He's got on a pair of casual jeans, which look tailored to fit around his anatomy. He has a tail with a puff of fur at the tip, and big, thick thighs with high hocks and dusty hooves. He doesn't wear shoes, but I didn't expect him to. They're sort of built-in.

His face is what most takes me by surprise. He has a broad snout with a black nose, and wide-set, dark eyes that immediately make him look kind and mellow. His pelt is coal black and shining, with just a stripe of white running up the bridge of his muzzle and over his eyebrows. There's another big patch of white down his throat and chest that fans out in a rather tantalizing manner under his shirt.

Stiffly he enters the room, and doesn't look at me until he's firmly sitting down on the couch kitty-corner from mine. His sheer weight squashes the cushions, and I can see the couch bottoming out underneath him.

When he finally does raise his eyes to mine, they are shy, and have shockingly long eyelashes.

"Hey," I say, not sure how else to greet him. "I'm Celeste."

He grunts and nods. "Theo," he says in answer. Then he sticks out a hand toward me, rather robotically, and it's big and calloused with super short fingernails. When I take it, my hand vanishes into his palm.

"Nice to meet you, Theo."

His eyes dart away from mine as he swallows and says, "It's good to meet you as well."

After this we both fall quiet, and I'm not sure what to say to fill the awkward void. Well, this is going great already. When I can't stand the silence anymore, I say, "So, tell me about yourself, Theo."

Surprised to hear me speak, his gaze darts up to mine. His eyes are farther apart than I'm accustomed to, separated by the flat ridge of his muzzle.

"Well..." His voice is deep, but somehow still quiet enough that I have to strain to hear him. "I'm Theo. But I guess you know that already. I, um, work in construction, and I have two dogs." He scratches the back of his head.

Right. All things he already put on his application.

"Do you have any hobbies, Theo?" I ask. This seems like a good, safe place to start. Aside from my daily chores working on the community garden, I have a lot of free time on my hands, so I've picked up drawing and painting. I think that Theo might be nice to paint.

"Oh. Um." He trails off. "I work a lot, so I don't have tons of time, but I really like to watch movies. Then I write a review for every movie I see."

So he's that guy. I wonder if I've read any of them. I always check the reviews before picking something out on Netflix.

"If you work a lot," I say carefully, "would you have time for me?"

Theo's eyes widen, and a muscle in his neck flexes. "Yes, of course," he says in a rush. "I would make time. I mean, I work a lot because, uh, I don't have much to do otherwise. Except for the movies thing. And I visit my grand-dam in the nursing home on the weekends."

This catches my interest. "Are you close with her?"

He nods. "After my folks died, she pretty much raised me."

Oh. Poor guy. "I'm sorry about your parents," I say. "That must have been really hard."

"That's all right." He shrugs. "It happened when I was young. I don't remember much about them."

"I'm glad you had your grandmother."

A smile tugs at the edges of his lips. "Me, too. I didn't want to put her in a home, but she needs more care than I can give her. So I try to visit as often as possible."

My heart warms. He's a caretaking type.

"What about you?" Theo asks. "What about your, um, parents?"

I wasn't really prepared for him to turn the question around on me. I guess for most people it isn't as complicated. "I was adopted," I say. "They left me at the compound when I was a baby."

This admission seems to take him by surprise. Theo leans forward, and his eyes soften. "You were left? Here?"

"I guess so." It's not really a wound so much anymore as it is an ache. "They must have done it for a good reason, though."

Not that I'll ever know what that reason was. All I know is two humans were somehow surviving outside the preserve.

They must have feared for the safety of their baby, and that's why they brought me here. I guess everyone in New Eden is a parent to me now. Julianne did the lion's share of the work raising me, though, and I still miss her every day.

Theo's eyebrows tilt with sympathy. "Not the kind of thing I thought we would have in common." I like how low and gentle his voice is.

"Me neither," I say. It is nice to have even a small point of connection.

Again we fall silent, and I'm not sure what to say next. This isn't going nearly as well as I'd hoped. Maybe I should end it now and let him get back to work, since I'm pretty sure I'll be wasting my time and his by trying to continue this conversation when he doesn't seem to have much interest in talking. Theo shifts uncomfortably on the small couch, his big haunches clearly making it awkward for him to sit so low to the ground.

"It's Celeste, right?" Theo says suddenly.

I blink at him. "Yes."

For a few seconds his eyes connect with mine, and then bashfully he looks away again. "That's a beautiful name."

It's so honest and gently spoken that the compliment stalls me for a moment. "Oh, thank you. One of the former administrators gave it to me. She said it sounded like *celestial*, and thought that was fitting. Like I had been sent down from the stars."

"A gift." When Theo smiles this time, I can see all of his flat upper teeth. It's a charming smile, if a tad uneasy, like he doesn't want to scare me off with it.

"I guess so." I shrug. "I've never felt like one, though."

His smile falls. "Why is that?"

Suddenly, I'm not sure how much to give away, or how honest I should be with someone I've just met. But his ears are flicked towards me, listening, and his deep eyes have no shred of judgment in them.

So I take a deep breath and say, "I wish I'd been born a monster." I press my hands between my thighs to still my nervousness. "Being human, I feel helpless. I can't even live on my own. I can't go to the movies, or the mall, or see a concert." There are so many experiences that are closed off to me, it feels like I only get to live one-sixth of a life. "New Eden is all I know, and that's only because monsters built it for us."

Theo's face is so open and expressive that I can see when he's overcome by sympathy. "I've never thought about what your life is like behind these walls," he says, tilting his head down. "I'm sorry. That must be hard."

I shrug. "I guess. It's never been any other way."

"You deserve more." I'm surprised to find Theo looking steadily at me. "Would you like to go sometime?"

"Go?" I sit up straight. "Where?"

"Go out somewhere, like to the movies. I could take you."

He wants to go on a date? That's rather baffling, as this whole conversation has made me feel like he'd be more comfortable anywhere else besides here with me. Going to see a movie in person sounds fun, though, even if it's with this shy minotaur who doesn't quite know how to make conversation. I'd finally get to see a new release before it hits video—and he's the one offering, so maybe I don't have to feel guilty about potentially wasting his time. Maybe he'll open up to me more, too.

Venturing out into the world, though, surrounded by monsters everywhere I look? I swallow hard. I'll be trusting Theo to keep me safe, to fight off any creature that might decide to make a meal of me.

"Okay," I finally say, my heart pounding. "I'd like that."

That smile returns to Theo's face, and it's even bigger this time. I decide that I like the way he smiles.

"Great. I'll pick you up, um, tomorrow night?" His tail flicks, and he grabs it to stop it. "If that's not too soon."

It's not like I have anything else going on.

"Sure." I find that, as I say it, I'm starting to feel excited. "Tomorrow night, then."

Chapter Three

"You have a date?" Maddie says over our Zoom call, her eyes as wide as plates. "You?"

"Yes, me."

She whistles. "I'm surprised. Usually you don't even look at your applications."

I don't want to tell her that it's partially because I'm envious of what she has with Egorr. I want someone to care for me, too, the way he does her. I want a partner to go to the movies with me, to make meals with me, to—

Maddie's voice cuts off my thought. "Who is it? What caught your interest?"

I explain about Theo the minotaur, who was so shy at our meeting that I'm still not quite sure what kind of person he is.

"Huh. I would have imagined someone outgoing for you," Maddie says. "But maybe you need someone who's more reserved in your life."

"It's too early for that, isn't it?" I ask. I'm trying not to set any expectations for Theo, so I won't be disappointed if he doesn't meet them. "This is just a get-to-know-you thing."

"Uh huh." It doesn't sound like she believes me. "So, what are you going to wear?"

Maddie makes me try on some clothes in front of the camera, and I twirl around with each new outfit, pulling my brown hair out of my face. But she *tsks* at every one. There's nothing in my wardrobe that really qualifies as "going out" clothes.

"At least keep your hair down," she says. "It's really hot."

I remember how Theo showed up to our meet-and-greet in jeans and a t-shirt, and wonder if I'm overthinking it. He's a guy who works outside, and it's not like I'm trying to impress him.

But maybe I am, just a tiny bit. I found it charming how even that big couch in the lounge was too small for him. I want to see him smile more.

"I might just go with this top and jeans," I say.

"That's so plain!" Maddie whines. "You want to impress him, don't you?"

"Not really." What I want is for him to see the real me, and let him decide if he likes it or not. "So what do you think of the blouse?"

Maddie sighs. "Wear whatever. But I hope you'll actually give this guy a chance, Celeste."

"I promise I'm going into it with an open mind." Besides, I liked Theo's big, dark eyes. I want to know what else is behind them. And I'm curious about what he'll show me out in the world.

While I wait by the security station on the edge of the preserve, I keep thinking about Theo. His deep voice, the way his tail danced when he got excited. I hope I'm more interesting this time.

Soon a truck drives up the isolated road that leads to New Eden, the muffler spitting as it approaches. By the looks of it, it's probably fifteen years old with 250,000 miles. A few exterior parts have been replaced over the years, and what's left has seen better days.

The truck comes to a stop in front of the compound. When Theo gets out, a burst of thrill shoots through me. It's been years since anyone picked me up for a date. I watch through the window as he talks to the guard, a big reptilian, who then radios through to us on the other side of the heavy steel door.

"It's Mr. Atlan, here for Celeste."

Theo is already holding open the truck door for me as I emerge from the building. When I'd met him in the lounge he was sitting down, but now that he's standing right in front of me, I realize just how tall he is—and how broad and beefy his shoulders are. *Is it tacky of me to think he's beefy?* His huge deltoids stretch his shirt across his chest in a way that's quite pleasing to look at, and his big, sturdy bear stomach is visible under there, too.

"It's, um, good to see you again," Theo says, tilting his head down rather steeply so he can get a good look at me.

I'm genuine when I answer, "You, too." He looks good. Better than good. He's like a lava cake, spilling over with delicious dark chocolate.

Theo holds the door while I climb into the truck. The vehicle's clearly been built for someone his size because I have to hop up onto the side step before I can even get to the seat. The cab is clean, even if the seats are a little worn out, and I could probably disappear into it.

The truck rocks as Theo closes my door, then climbs in the driver's side. He puts it in gear and soon we're trundling down the two-lane road that leads away from the preserve. I'm elated.

"The movie's at 7:30," Theo says, heading towards the

highway. The sun is getting in his eyes, so he squints and lowers the visor. "I just picked something out I thought you might like."

I wonder what information I gave him during our first short meeting to inform this decision.

"Okay, cool," I say, trying to sound light and airy. "I'm happy with whatever." I do my best not to fiddle with my hands while the truck motors on. I'm curious which movie he's chosen, and what it means about his first impression of me.

Again that awkward quiet falls. Theo's big hands squeeze the steering wheel, his brow furrowed like he's thinking hard. I wonder what internal monologue has him so concentrated. Is there something he wants to say but isn't saying?

Time passes and still, nothing.

"Do you want to put on some music?" I ask, hoping that might help fill the silence.

Theo jolts at the sound of my voice. "Oh, sure!" With a sigh of relief, he reaches for the knob and presses it.

Immediately, I'm blasted by an explosion of noise. A guitar screams, and someone is shouting into a mic in a deep, growly voice. The car veers off to the left as Theo, overcome by panic, reaches to turn down the volume. He cranks the knob back to zero and just as suddenly as the onslaught began, the car falls silent again.

Theo rights the wheel and sits back up, panting. He keeps his gaze straight ahead, his back ram-rod straight.

"Sorry." He scratches the back of his neck, looking deeply uncomfortable. "That was just, uh—"

"It's fine," I say, waving a hand. If anything, I find it amusing, even enlightening. So when he's alone, Theo likes to listen to death metal? I've learned something useful today. He's not quite what I expected. "What band is it?" I ask, gesturing at the silent radio.

His big, long head turns slightly, eyebrows raised. "Oh, they're called Killer Jester." He swallows. "You probably haven't heard of them, though. They're kind of niche."

I don't personally listen to death metal on the regular, but I know it exists. I like metal that's a little less intense. Sometimes it helps me paint to put some on in my earbuds and go to town.

"Haven't heard of them," I say. "But they sound cool." I'd listen to death metal with him if he wanted. Theo nods, but doesn't say anything else, clearly still rattled. I need to think of something that will draw out this conversation a little longer, so I add, "I've listened to The Hand, though."

Theo's face brightens. "I like them a lot, too. They're more mainstream, but I don't mind that if it gets new people excited about the music." He's talking about it with a surprising amount of passion. I haven't seen this much enthusiasm out of him about anything yet, so I decide to dig a little deeper.

"You like music?" I ask. I want to learn more. Perhaps having some common interests would make it less awkward between us.

"Sure." Theo seems ever-so-slightly more comfortable, his big hands gripping the wheel less tightly. "I always have music playing, when I can. Listening to that kind of stuff really relaxes me."

Huh. Who would have thought that somebody screaming bloody murder into a microphone would be relaxing? I guess everyone has their thing.

"So you do have other hobbies!" I grin to show that I'm teasing. "Number one: Movies. Number two: Listening to death metal."

Theo chuckles, and it's the first time I think I've heard him laugh. It's easy and light and I find I want a lot more of it. "I guess so. Two hobbies, then."

After a while I switch the music back on, gently turning

down the volume until it's at a more reasonable level, and I even bang my head to it, earning an amused snort from Theo. Eventually we reach town, and though I've passed through the city in a car before, the shadows of such tall buildings still take me by surprise. There are so many creatures bustling about in all shapes and sizes. A huge cyclops crosses an intersection on a green light, and Theo has to slam on the brakes. The cyclops cusses at him, lifting his huge arms and roaring at us like a bear. I shrink back into my seat as the cyclops jogs to the other side of the road. Theo shakes his head.

"Close one, big guy," he mutters. Then he turns down the music so I can hear him. "I didn't think to ask you. What are your hobbies?"

I'm pleased that he's asking me a question about myself. Maybe he does want to get to know me, but just forgets that he needs to initiate the conversation.

"Well, I try to be cool and take my canvas and easel out into some beautiful, natural place to paint landscapes," I say. I'd always liked those old children's books with the gorgeous watercolor backgrounds. "But the best we have on the preserve is the river they built through the middle, and I can't actually paint for shit like that because my water is always falling over. So now I just find a good photo and paint in my house like a civilized person." Theo listens raptly as he finds his way into the parking lot of the movie theater.

"I don't think it matters where you're painting from as long as you're enjoying yourself," he says as he turns off the truck. "That's what living is all about."

I think I like that outlook. He seems to be the sort of person who exists in the now and isn't too harsh of a critic about it.

As we walk up to the theater together, I'm dwarfed by Theo's shadow. To open the door, all he has to do is reach over my head and his immense arm pushes it wide enough for me to step through. I feel like a child next to him, the top of my head only reaching his pectorals. He could probably scoop me up without trying and carry me all the way to the peak of a mountain.

I find I enjoy the idea of that, being picked up by him and carried like a kid. Nothing could touch me there.

After he buys us tickets, we get right in line for snacks. I keep close to him as monsters walk past us and make it clear to the two naga waiting behind us in line that I'm accounted for. By the time we make it to the theater we're each carrying a bucket of popcorn with a box of Milk Duds balanced on top. Theo sucks on a Mountain Dew.

"Do you always eat like this?" I ask as we enter the theater, finding seats at the very back so Theo's horns won't block anyone's view.

"Just at the movies." He clears his throat, as if nervous I'll judge him for it. "It's special. Especially this time."

A warmth washes over me when he says it. *I'm special.* I'm starting to wonder if his quiet awkwardness is just a natural feature and has nothing to do with me.

The movie Theo's picked is about a concert violinist working her way up from childhood poverty to playing first chair in a world-class orchestra. He was right in choosing it. My eyes well up with tears at least three times, and by the big climax of the movie, I'm outright crying. As humiliating as it is to ugly-cry on a first date, I just can't help it.

A hand lightly brushes my skin. Startled, I look up to find Theo reaching over the armrest to rub up and down my arm in a soothing motion. It's unexpected, but so gentle that I let myself cry a little bit harder because now I'm pretty sure he won't judge me.

When I'm finally recovered and the movie is winding down, I lean and rest my temple on Theo's big bicep. For a moment he tenses up, and I wonder if I've overstepped. But then he relaxes, even adjusting his arm to slide it over my shoulder and bring me in closer to his chest. I'm having a strangely wonderful time crying in the darkness next to Theo.

As the credits take over, we sit there in silence, watching white text scroll across the screen until the lights come on. Finally, we get up to leave. I realize that this time the quiet between us was comfortable, companionable, with a familiar easiness to it. On the way out, Theo takes my leftover Milk Duds and pours the rest into his mouth.

"Is there anything else you want to do before we head back?" he asks as we approach the truck.

Anything else I want to do? Is he asking me to come over? Surely it's a little soon for that—and anyway, this is shy Theo we're talking about. He would never proposition me after just one date. He must see my surprise because he adds, "We could get some coffee, or ice cream, or something like that. Whatever you want to do that you can't do at New Eden."

We did just spend two hours sitting quietly next to each other in the dark, and I wouldn't mind some real, quality time getting to know him. Now that he's starting to unfurl in front of me, to show me little bits and pieces of his real self, I want to see what comes out next. He has a soft side, I know this for certain. So what else is in there?

"Ice cream sounds great," I say, voting to prolong our time together. Even though I just ate half a box of Milk Duds, something about going to the soda fountain together sounds like a sweet teenage date I didn't get to have.

"Great. I know the perfect place."

Chapter Four

When we get to Fifteen Flavors, "the best ice cream shop in the whole city," Theo reaches over my head to open the door for me again. This time, he's much closer to my backside, and I get a powerful whiff of him. He wears the kind of demure deodorant that somebody who actually works all day would use, but it can't quite cover the warm, musky, natural smell of him. He gently brushes my back with one hand to guide me inside.

He pays for my ice cream, too, and I object. I get a small allowance for outings like this, and since I never go on them, I've built up a pretty sturdy savings.

"That's what I asked for, isn't it?" he says, gently guiding me to a table with a hand at my lower back. "Someone I could spoil?"

That is true, and it's one of the reasons I chose him. I wanted to feel cared for in whatever relationship I have. "Yes, you did," I admit.

"Then that's what I'm going to do," he says firmly. "For as long as you'll let me."

Something about those words brings a soft, steady warmth to my chest. Maybe it's just our first date, but I'm starting to understand Theo more every moment. If he wants to keep spoiling me after this, then I'll most certainly let him.

We sit down next to each other at the tiny table, and he licks up his ice cream with his huge, pink tongue. What would kissing him be like with that tongue? Just the thought of it sends a shiver down my arms. I wonder if maybe, back at New Eden, he'll try to kiss me. I hope he does. My belly tingles just imagining it.

I'm like a teenage girl with a first crush.

There's that awkward silence again, so I decide to break it with a question. A rather bold one.

"How are you still single?" I ask. Theo might be shy at first, but he's a catch. He's in his mid-thirties and stable. He should have been plucked off eons ago.

His eyes widen, and he pauses licking up his ice cream. "Well, uh, I..." His shoulders tense up. "I don't know. Maybe I don't put myself out there?"

"But you sent in an application," I say. "That's certainly putting yourself out there, isn't it?"

He shrinks down a little. "I didn't think I'd get picked. Being, well, a minotaur and everything."

So he submitted his application not really intending on going out with me? I find that I'm hurt by this. I thought that after what he said he was serious about finding a human partner. "So you sent it in on a whim?" I ask, trying not to let my emotions seep into my voice, but I can't help it.

A look of panic flashes over Theo's face. "Oh, no. Not at all." He reaches for my hand instinctively, and it disappears into his huge palm. He squeezes, and there's a fear in his eyes that he's just royally fucked things up. "Actually, I agonized over that application for days. I didn't want to say what I thought you'd want to hear. Everything I wrote is true." He huffs out a breath. "I wanted more than anything to get to meet you. I really did."

His sincerity almost bowls me over. I squeeze his hand back to show him that I'm not upset. "Do I live up to the hype?" I ask, jokingly.

But Theo's very serious. "You are wonderful, Celeste. When your heart broke during the movie, mine broke with it." The way he looks at me with those big dark eyes, meaning every word he says, I feel like a candle melting into a puddle. I lean just a little closer to him, because all I want is to be touching even more.

"How did you know I would like that one so much?" I ask. "You just guessed."

He shrugs his huge shoulders. "I think you have a big heart. It seemed like the kind of thing that would move you."

Right. I forgot that he writes movie reviews. He would know how to pick a movie out for me. I don't know if I agree about the *huge heart* business, but coming from him it feels like a compliment.

"Thank you." I wind my hand up his arm, around his big bicep. "It was fun spending time with you tonight." I'm not afraid to say it. I think someone like Theo, someone who's earnest and shy, should hear that he's great from time to time.

He scratches the back of his head again, that nervous gesture I've already started to find adorable. "I've had a great time, too," he says. "You're a lot of fun." If I'm learning anything about Theo, it's that he's always sincere, so I believe him. Suddenly he asks, "Do you want to go out again?" There's a vulnerable uncertainty in the question.

Both of our ice creams have liquefied now. For the first time, we've been so engaged in talking that everything else has faded into the background.

"Yes!" It comes out a little louder and more enthusiastic than I intended, so I lower my voice. "Of course. I'd love that." My heart is racing at top speed just thinking about spending more time with him and touching even more of him.

"Great," Theo says, smiling wide enough to show both rows of his flat teeth. "I know a spot with fantastic Indian food."

That's not something we get often on the preserve, and I sure can't wait to find out more about him—to unravel all the layers of him. "Let's do it."

When the truck pulls up to the high walls of New Eden, I let myself out and meet Theo in front of the glowing headlights. Our shadows are cast long and tall, though his still dwarfs mine.

"Thank you," I say. As we stand in front of each other, my hand finds its way into his. I like how natural it feels just to hold his big fingers in mine. "For taking me out."

This is the moment. If he wants to kiss me, dropping me off at what is essentially my parents' doorstep is the time to do it. But Theo doesn't take me in his arms, and there's a stiffness to him like he's not sure what to do next. I want him to come a step closer, and then another step still. I want to smell his deodorant again.

"You asked me why I'm still single." He rubs a thumb over the back of my hand anxiously. "It's because I don't make the move. I don't say what I want. I don't know how."

Oh, so that's it. I decide in that moment that it's up to me to be bold. "Well, I can tell you right now what *I* want."

Theo's gaze jumps to mine, and he nods eagerly. "Yes. Please tell me."

"I want you to kiss me." There, I've said it.

His nostrils flare. Then he inhales deeply, like he's preparing for something, and it musses some of my hair.

"Happily," he says.

When Theo leans down, his soft, warm body is still farther away than I would like, so I reach for his hips and pull him towards me. But I want to let him initiate, so I wait patiently until he finally sweeps up my lips in his.

His mouth is much bigger than mine, and shaped very differently, but somehow he's still delicate with it. I find his arms winding around my back, bringing me in closer as we explore each other. He teases my lips with his tongue, and oh, that tongue. It's wide and thick, with a rough texture I didn't expect. The feel of it in my mouth makes me gasp and Theo's arms tighten around me at the sound. I meet his tongue with mine and quickly, our chaste kiss becomes something different, more urgent, more lavish. Even as I'm dwarfed by him and his huge muzzle, I'm floating in him, too. It occurs to me that he's not inexperienced if he can kiss this way. He may be shy on the surface, but there's clearly much more to him. His hand splays across my hip, brushing my ass, and instinctively my body presses into his. Theo answers with a grunt, and suddenly he pulls his mouth away from mine.

I blink a few times, clearing away the haze I was just in. Theo is panting, his pupils gigantic, and he runs a hand roughly through his hair.

"Sorry," he says. "I got carried away." He seems embarrassed—ashamed that we got so into it.

"Don't be sorry. I liked it." My fingers dance down his arm, then squeeze into the soft caress of his hand again. "I really liked it."

I think if he weren't covered in fur he might be blushing right now, but the way he turns his head and coughs gets it across. I like that he let go just a small amount, that kissing me drew him in and unlocked some of his more instinctive urges.

I kiss Theo one more time, a playful peck that makes him chuckle, before he gets in the truck and drives away. In the distance, I can hear death metal roaring through the open window.

~

After my date, it's as if all of my nerve endings have been put into overdrive. I'm still feeling his ghost touches even as I lie in bed, trying to sleep.

I'm not just excited for our next date. I'm *thrilled*. It took some coaxing to bring out a snapshot of the authentic Theo, but now I know it's there, peeking out at me.

He clearly liked me, too. He wanted me when we kissed, and it fills my head with soft fuzzies. I've never felt wanted that way before.

My brain's too occupied with Theo to fall asleep, so I pull out a toy from my bedside table. Sure, we've only had one date, but I'm already curious what Theo's packing under those fitted jeans. He's a massive guy, so I can't imagine his, erm, jewels are any less significant.

It's easy to hit my peak thinking about that textured tongue stroking mine, and imagining where else it could go.

~

Maddie is more than excited when I tell her that we have a second date already planned. I'm trying to keep my expectations low, but it's harder when she's bouncing up and down like a little kid who had too much cake.

"I knew you would find someone if you just tried," Maddie says over the Zoom call, with an annoying, smug smile.

"It was Rob who convinced me."

She huffs. "I tried to first! It's like loosening up a jar. I take partial credit for starting the ball rolling."

"I don't want to get too excited yet," I say, and I think I'm telling myself more than anything. "I don't know where this is headed." And there's always the threat when you get close to a monster that they'll flip a switch one day and decide you're dinner. It's only happened once, as typically it's creatures who have control of themselves who apply for a human companion, then they're carefully vetted by the relationship coordinator before they meet us.

I don't think that would be Theo, but we barely know each other. I don't want to get my hopes up.

Maddie arches an eyebrow, unimpressed.

"Look, Celeste. I know it's easy to wall yourself off." Now she speaks with a little more tenderness. "But I hope you'll put yourself out there and give him a chance. You already look happier."

She's probably right. I didn't realize how great it was to have something to look forward to. It energizes my steps, even makes my food taste better.

"Let yourself get whisked away," Maddie tells me. "You're very whiskable."

Chapter Five

Theo's set to pick me up for our second date a few days later. Every hour until he arrives feels longer than the last one, and I'm annoyed at how anxious and excited I am, like it's my first day of school.

Jeez. This is what happens when you don't date enough.

Soon the truck comes rumbling down the road. I wait behind the door with the guard until it comes to a stop and Theo gets out.

The moment I see him, I want him to hold me again like he did the other night. The way his huge hands grabbed onto me was divine. I wonder if a greeting hug is within the realm of acceptable at this stage.

It turns out I don't have to worry about it because when I jog out, Theo's arms are open wide and waiting for me. He looks genuinely pleased to see me as my hands wind their way around his middle and I bury my face in his soft chest. He smells like soap and detergent—he must have just showered and put on some fresh clothes to take me out. It makes me feel like I'm important to him.

After a moment, we awkwardly disentangle ourselves, and I don't wait for him to open the truck door for me. It's tricky to reach the handle and close it once I'm inside, but I manage.

"Sorry," Theo says. "I should've gotten that for you."

I wave him off. "I can open a car door. I'll have to figure it out eventually." I regret it immediately because it's presumptuous to say I'll be riding in this truck again. But when I turn to look at him, Theo's just smiling.

"I think you'll get the hang of it quick." With a chuckle, he puts the truck in drive and we head into town. This time he's playing regular metal, and I roll down my window to let it blast. Partway through the drive, Theo reaches over and squeezes my thigh—just one brief gesture to show me he's having a good time even while we're not talking.

Just entering the Indian restaurant is a feast for my senses. The walls are beautiful and covered in murals, and the air is rich and succulent with spices. Monsters chatter all around us.

"Celeste?" Theo asks, holding a chair he's pulled out for me while I daydream. The hostess, a harpy with long, red fingernails, waits for me to sit so she can give us our menus.

"Sorry," I say as I slide into it. But Theo is grinning.

"Have you been to a restaurant before?" he asks, taking the much bigger seat they've provided for him on the other side of the table.

I shake my head. "Coffee shop," I say. "Last time I went anywhere, it was to a coffee shop." It wasn't a very productive date, and all I got out of it was a peppermint latte and a croissant. "That was a few years ago."

He glances up at me, eyebrows raised. "That's the last time you left New Eden?"

It must seem pretty strange to an outsider. "I don't really date," I say.

Theo blinks a few times, showing off his long lashes. "Oh. But you went on one with me?"

"You're the exception, I guess." I study the menu, not really reading any of the words because it's hard to look him in the eyes while we have this conversation. "I saw your application and I just... It spoke to me."

Silence stretches out between us before I finally glance up. There's a rather goofy smile on Theo's face as he says, "I'm really happy you picked me."

When the waitress comes back, he orders every vegetarian dish on the menu for us. I've never seen so much food in my life, but he assures me that we'll finish it all. He's not kidding, either—he inhales it like a vacuum cleaner, and I'm not sure where it all goes. This must be how he fuels that huge body of his. Every single dish is incredible, an absolute party for my tastebuds.

I'm so full afterwards that as we walk out, I feel like I could sit down and fall asleep. Theo laughs as I take his arm.

"You'll have to carry me back to the car." I moan melodramatically. "I can barely move."

In an instant, Theo scoops me up into his arms, and I let out a squeal of surprise. I didn't expect him to actually do it. But it's just like I'd fantasized, and he barely strains a muscle supporting my extra weight.

"I can do that," he says with a wink, and without much effort he carries me back to the truck. I'm blushing furiously, and a pair of manticores stare at us as we pass. Theo hefts most of my weight into one arm as he opens the door with the other hand, then sets me in the passenger seat tenderly, like I'm a doll he might break. While he's leaned over me, he bends down and pecks me on the lips.

I'm too shocked by the spontaneity of it all to kiss him back before he's closing the door and walking around to the driver's seat.

So he does have an outgoing side. A fun, sweet, playful side. I rub my lips, wondering where this new Theo came from.

I like it.

After dinner, Theo invites me to a little bar so we can get a drink. This feels like the more serious, adult version of getting ice cream. We've graduated. Then it'll be time for me to go home.

Home. The preserve. Now that I've been in the outside world—twice now—I find that I don't want to go back. Out here, everything is alive. The food is fantastic, and I find I don't worry about the other monsters around as much as I thought I would. It feels full of color and life in a way that New Eden just isn't.

When we reach the bar, Theo is quiet at first, as I'm finding he usually is until he finds his footing. I wait for him to settle in as he takes a long sip of his drink.

Finally he asks, "Why did you choose me, Celeste?"

That came out of nowhere. I'm not even sure I know how to answer.

"Maybe it sounds cliche," I say uncertainly, "but in your picture, you looked... sweet. Like you would be a kind person. Or, uh, minotaur." He'd seemed trustworthy right away, and I believed his answers to the questions. Plus, he looked really hot with his bare chest under his bright orange safety jacket.

"Oh, that picture." He runs a hand down his face with a groan. "I forgot about that. One of my coworkers insisted I go shirtless. He wanted it to look like, what is it? One of those fire-fighter calendars?"

That explains the look on his face in the photo, a combination of sultry and awkward. I laugh.

"Well, it worked on me," I say. Not to mention that really big lump in his pants.

His eyebrows go up. "You liked it?"

"I sure did. But I also liked what you said. About, um..." My face is starting to get hot. "About wanting someone to spoil. About wanting to make a home."

There, I've said it. I've put the idea into the air that maybe I could be that person. My heart is racing as Theo takes this in, his lips parted.

"Is that what you want, too?" he asks tentatively. His expression is wide open to me now, nervous but also hopeful, and there's a sincerity to him that makes my heart swell.

"Yeah. I think I do." No, I *know* I do. But I don't want to seem too eager because that would also make me vulnerable. "I really like you, Theo. A lot."

He chokes on his drink, then starts coughing. He bangs one fist on his chest, and I pat his back as he coughs a few more times.

"Do I need to do the Heimlich?" I ask, worried. "I think you might be too big for me to do it."

Theo chuckles, and it makes him cough again. "No, no, I'm fine." He wipes his mouth with a cocktail napkin. "I've just never been with someone as forward as you." His grin is wide and sweet, and his ears tilt down in that way that means he's pleased. "I like it. You tell me what you want and how you feel, so then I feel more comfortable saying it, too."

I take in the way he's shyly curled around his drink, which looks funny when he's more than seven feet tall and three hundred pounds of muscle, and my affection for him swells. I like his wide horns that he somehow manages to maneuver everywhere without bonking them. I'm interested in his big furry haunches, which taper down into big, dusty black hooves.

"I never thought being forward was a bonus until now," I say with a chuckle. "Most people think I'm too candid."

Theo shakes his head insistently. "No, it's great. I really like you, too, you know." Then he opens his mouth like he's about to say something else, but decides against it.

"What is it?" I ask, leaning towards him. I mimic his gesture from last time and stroke his arm. "You can tell me."

He relaxes under my hand. "I was going to ask if you wanted to, um..." He lets out a sharp breath as he gathers his courage. "If you wanted to try it out. Get off the preserve and, you know, move in with me."

A trial marriage. A test to see if it would work out long-term, before we go any further with this. Then we can spend more time together, and he can show me that he'll offer me a good home. As the human in the situation, I can say "no" any time I want and return to New Eden, no questions asked. I'll have my own space in the house that's reserved for me and only me.

I like the idea of seeing what sort of home Theo would create.

"Yes." I don't have to think twice about it. I sit up as high as I can on the bar stool so I can kiss his cheek. "I would really like that."

Theo exhales with relief, and winds one arm around my waist. His hand is gentle but still firm, and now that it's touched me there, I want it to touch even more places. I imagine being alone in his house, doing more than just kissing, and I wriggle a little on the bar stool as my lower body gets the message.

"Great," Theo says with a beaming smile, not realizing

what he's doing to me. "I think you'll like it. And I know Bug and Ramona will like you, too."

I nestle into his big armpit. "I'm so excited to meet your dogs."

When we head back to New Eden that night, I'm eager to go inside and start the paperwork, but I don't want to leave Theo quite so soon.

"Will you be back tomorrow night?" I ask. Part of me worries that he'll change his mind, decide it's too quick, and back out.

"Don't worry." He leans down and kisses my forehead. "I'll be back tomorrow, and then we'll get to see each other every day." His lips traverse down my cheek to brush over my mouth, just a tease. It makes me hungry for more. Soon our tongues are playing together, his big one looping around my small one. He reaches behind me and holds me up by my butt so our faces can be closer together, and my toes lift off the ground.

One of the security guards clears his throat, and we abruptly separate. Theo lets out an awkward laugh and heads back to the truck.

"I'll see you tomorrow," he says.

When he drives away, I hope that it'll be the last time he leaves without me.

Chapter Six

Rob stands at my door while I pack up most of my everyday things, leaning against the frame.

"Just two dates, huh?" he says, waggling an eyebrow at me. "It must be going well with the minotaur."

"His name is Theo." I click my makeup case shut and add it to the suitcase. The resident coordinator had to give me one because I didn't own any luggage, having no reason to use any before. I look down at it with affection, wondering what sort of places Theo and I might go together where I could bring a suitcase along. "And yeah, it is going well. He was shy at first, but I think I'm starting to crack the nut."

For someone so reserved, I'm surprised at how affectionate he is, how sensual and charged his kisses are. And he is the one who asked me to do the trial, after all. He knew what he wanted, and he said it. That feels like a powerful step forward.

"Hmm." Rob watches me fold up clothes and add them to the pile and cracks a smile. "I'm glad you gave him a chance, Celeste."

I am, too.

"But there's no way to know how it will go," I say, rummaging around my bathroom. I'm not sure if he'll have shampoo and conditioner. He must, to keep his pelt so shiny and smooth. It was soft as silk under my hands. "I'm trying not to get my hopes up too high."

"Why not?" Rob asks. "Hope can be a helpful thing. You should go into it open to the idea that it *will* work out."

"What if something happens?" I stop packing and turn to him. "What if he's one of those minotaurs with a temper? What if a switch flips and he tramples me?"

Rob blinks. "He's not going to trample you, Celeste."

I shut the suitcase. "You just never know."

I don't pack up everything because I'm not moving out of my house on the preserve yet. But despite what I said, it feels like a huge door has opened up for me and I'm eager to walk through it.

The next day is a Friday, and Theo is waiting for me in front when I wheel out my suitcases. He helps me load them in the back of his truck. Before we can part ways to hop in, he takes me by the hand, leans down, and gives me a quick kiss.

"I can't wait to do this with you," he says, just for my ears.

I shudder at the tickle of his breath. "Me, too."

Then we hop into the truck, and we're off.

I'm surprised when we don't drive into town. Instead, Theo takes an exit that leads us off into the countryside, up and down a few hills until we reach a small suburb. He pulls into the driveway of a yellow house with red shutters, a modest two-story with a wooden fence all the way around a big backyard. There are some pots out front with half-living plants in them, and right away I decide my first task will be bringing them back to life.

Theo catches my eye and does his trademark scratch at

the back of his neck as he carries in my luggage without breaking a sweat. "Yeah, I'm not really a green thumb. But if you are…"

"I love plants. I take care of the garden in New Eden." I hope that Rob will be able to handle it without me.

"Oh, awesome." Theo brightens up as he gestures around us. "Build a garden. Anywhere you want. I'll get the compost, and I can make you some gardening boxes with scrap wood from the work site."

It would be like bringing a little bit of the preserve here with me. He's inviting me to leave a mark on his house and make it mine, too.

"I'd love that," I say, and he beams.

When we reach the door I hear barking, which quickly changes to whining when the dogs realize their owner is home. The door opens and immediately both dogs squeeze out, wagging and jumping and licking me all over.

"Bug, stay down," Theo says, but the big yellow dog can't be stopped. He's up on his back legs, sniffing my face, while the other one, Ramona, spins around in circles.

Eventually, we get my backpack and a few bags inside. His living room is clean, if a little cluttered. There are stands full of DVDs everywhere I look. He has a big TV mounted on the wall with tall, fancy-looking speakers.

As he leads me to the stairs, I realize the entertainment system is the most modern part of the house. The floors are beige linoleum and the cupboards are a 1970s green. But the house is cozy and has lots of warm light, and the kitchen sink looks out over the backyard. For a moment I think it's sad that we'll never get to have kids that I could watch play from the kitchen window, but dogs are just as good. Less upkeep.

"You'll be up here." Theo leads the way up the stairs and down a narrow hall. He stops at one of the three doors. "In the left one. Over there is your bathroom." He gestures at the door that's halfway open.

Right. That's the agreement—I get my own space, and he won't pressure me to sleep anywhere except my own bed. The trial rules say he can't come into the room without my permission. Not that he ever would.

Inside the room he's given me, I find a cute full-size bed with a brand new, flower-patterned comforter and matching pillows. There's a quaint desk wedged into a corner, too, with a fancy blue desk lamp. A few pictures hang on the wall—a pair of birds, a mountain landscape, a barn with two cows out front. The cows strike me as funny in a minotaur's house, and I wonder if Theo picked it for that reason.

"It's lovely," I say, dropping my backpack on the desk. I fall onto the bed and it's pillowy soft. Theo stands at the door, watching me with a wide, lopsided smile. "Did you do all of this for me?"

"Of course. It was just storage before." He lets out a shy *huff*. "I always hoped I'd be able to share it with someone."

I get up and jog over to him, wrapping my arms around his middle. Theo's surprised at first, but then he holds me tight against him.

"Thank you." I bury my face in his chest. "This means a lot to me."

He rests his chin on the top of my head. "I want you to feel happy and safe here. Whatever it takes."

We spend the whole weekend together, and it's like one long date where we never have to say goodbye at the end. Saturday morning, Theo takes me to the farmer's market—a concept I've heard about in passing, but never experienced.

It's bright and noisy, and everything smells amazing. There are piles of vegetables on tabletops, and ice chests boasting big steaks and cuts of ribs. I keep my distance from other monsters as they pass by us, and retreat into Theo's side when they get too close. Despite his presence so close to me, I can't help imagining a reanimated corpse taking a bite out of me. But I find Theo's big hand has woven around my shoulders, keeping me tight against him and protected.

Little food trucks at the end of the aisles sell everything from tacos to chicken satay, and I wish I could try something from each one. Theo chuckles at my enthusiasm. "We can come back every weekend, if you want," he says. "Until you've had them all."

It's a delicious feeling to know this isn't my only chance, and I don't have to worry about wasting it. Theo will bring me here again.

I settle on a simple burger and fries, and we sit down at some picnic tables near a sphinx and her apparent date, a gorgon with wiggling hair. I scoot a little closer to Theo, imagining of one of those snakes lashing out and sinking its fangs into me.

It's only once I'm halfway through my burger that I wonder if I've made a huge faux pas. "Is it weird?" I ask meekly. "That I'm eating, um, beef?"

It takes a few seconds for my question to register, and then Theo lets out a surprisingly boisterous laugh. The whole picnic table shakes. "No, no. Not at all." He wipes at one of his eyes, still snorting. I notice he lets out cute little *whuff*s like this sometimes, the way a farm animal might. "I don't like eating meat myself, but that's a personal preference. It's not because I have some secret kinship with cows or anything."

I let out a breath of relief. "Good. I didn't want you

thinking I'd try to eat you for dinner, or anything like that." The double entendre falls from my lips before I can stop it.

He laughs even harder, and it's the most animated I've seen him yet. I thought such an open overture would scandalize him. "Maybe I should cook you burgers at home," he says. "If you're so keen. They make really good ones with black beans."

"I'll try anything once," I say.

As Theo watches me finish my meal with his head propped up on one arm, there's a warm affection in his eyes. "You're really cute, Celeste," he says.

I freeze up completely. No one's said anything like that to me before.

"Oh, um." I rub my cheeks, trying to stave off the heat creeping into them. "Thank you."

He chuckles. "You're even cuter when you blush."

I'm still buzzing when we get home with all our new fresh produce. Theo isn't a gourmet by any means, but he can cut up vegetables without too much instruction, and actually has an array of spices in the cupboard. After dinner, we watch a movie from his massive collection: a fun rom-com that makes me feel fuzzy and warm. As the drama unfolds, Theo puts his arm around my shoulders and I snuggle up against his chest. Soon my hand finds its way to his knee because I want to feel even more of our bodies touching. I relish how his big breaths lift his chest under my head, how I can hear the beating of his huge heart while a sad song plays on the TV. When the hero and heroine kiss, I find I want nothing more than to kiss Theo, too, and show him just how much I enjoyed our day together.

When the movie's over, we remain on the couch while the credits roll, as if both of us are unwilling to call it a night already. Eventually we get up, and Theo holds my hand as we go up the stairs together.

Once we're standing in the hallway outside my door, Theo rubs the back of his head. "I suppose it's good night."

"I had a really fun day with you today," I say, taking a step closer to him.

His smile is big, showing both rows of his flat, white teeth. "Me, too." His hand finds its way to my hip, just dancing over the outside of my shirt and jeans. "You're so happy and curious." He leans down towards me. "Seeing you have fun gets me excited, too. And I think I really needed that." His other hand rises to my chin, and he tilts it up as his big, black nose drops down to mine.

The bare need to kiss him takes me over, and I rise up onto my toes to press my lips to his. Theo returns my enthusiasm, his tongue more adventurous than last time as it explores my mouth. When he nibbles my lips, a heady heat rises in my abdomen, urging me closer and closer to his soft body.

Finally we pull away, both of us panting, and I can see a thick lump has developed under Theo's jeans. It's huge, and my heart leaps into my throat at the sight of it—at the implication that I turn him on.

"Good night," Theo says, kissing my forehead. I think about inviting him into my room, but I'm not sure if either of us is ready yet. When it happens, I want it to feel exactly right.

"Good night."

Bug insists on sleeping on my bed with me, and I drift off wondering what it would be like to sleep next to Theo instead.

Chapter Seven

On Sundays, Theo tells me, he visits his grand-dam in the nursing home. She's just starting to lose her memory, forgetting small details about the past, confusing events, and struggling to use her cell phone. She has a difficult time getting place to place and needs around-the-clock care to help her eat and get to the bathroom. It's more than Theo could provide for her alone.

I'm surprised when he asks me to come along.

"You want me to meet her?" I ask at the table during breakfast. Theo's put together some french toast and eggs, with homemade whipped cream and fresh strawberries we got at the farmer's market yesterday.

His face falls a little. "Do you think it's too soon?" he asks. "Damn, you're probably right. You've only just moved in, and we haven't really talked about..."

I put a hand on his arm to slow him down. "I'm not refusing," I say. "I'm flattered you want to introduce me."

Theo lets out a heavy gust of air. "Oh. Phew." Jokingly, he

wipes his forehead of sweat. "I didn't want to jump the gun or anything."

"No, no. You didn't. I'd be more than happy to go with you." The idea of meeting the closest thing Theo has to a parent makes me nervous, but I want to be a part of his life, and his grand-dam is clearly important to him. "Do you want to bring her anything?"

His eyebrows jump. "Bring her something? Like what?"

I pick up the vase where we put the fresh sunflowers we bought at the market yesterday. "What if we take her flowers? I bet she doesn't get a lot of that at the nursing home."

Theo's eyes light up. "That's a great idea." He hands me the vase. "You carry this, okay? And we'll bring her new ones next weekend."

There's a fresh bounce in his step as we get into the truck together, the vase tucked between my knees, and head off.

The hallway of the nursing home has a comforting smell that reminds me of Julianne. Her home always smelled like this, and I think it will be nice to meet Theo's grand-dam. I hope I impress her.

I hold onto my minotaur's hand as he leads me down to number 207, where he stops and knocks on the door.

"Who is it?" a voice calls out. I hear a gasp as he steps inside. "Theo!"

"Not just me," he says as I walk in behind him. "I brought someone."

Inside is a cute, cozy apartment, with a bed by the window and a TV playing in the corner. Theo's grand-dam appears to have been watching old Westerns before we arrived, but she hurriedly turns down the sound as we enter.

She's mostly white with a few speckles of brown, and has a pink nose with long, gray hair braided down her shoulder. She has the same horns as Theo, but smaller and daintier. Her mouth falls open when she sees me.

"A human?" she asks, staring openly.

"I told you I sent in an application," he reminds her. "Remember when I took her on a date last week?"

"Oh, yes!" I'm not sure by her answer that she actually remembers, or if she's just pretending to remember. "Of course. What was her name again, Theo?"

He grins. "Celeste. And this is my grand-dam, Daphne." The hand around my waist tightens, and he stands up straight. "Celeste moved in this week."

Daphne covers her mouth. "Wow! So you're going ahead with the, um, what did you call it?"

"Trial marriage," Theo prompts.

She nods. "Right, of course. So you must get on well, then?"

Theo glances down at me, and I think I'm supposed to answer.

"We do," I say, with surprising certainty. "Theo is taking very good care of me. We're going to build a garden, and I love his two dogs."

He grins. "They love you just as much, I think."

Daphne claps her hands together. "Oh, that's fabulous. I'm so pleased to see you happy, Theo." She pats the chair next to her. "Both of you sit down. Celeste, I want to hear all about you. Tell me how you met Theo."

It's not a long story, but Daphne *ooh*s and *ahh*s at just the right moments when I talk about how I got his application, our two dates, and how Theo welcomed me into his home. I don't tell her about all the kissing, of course. I try not to think about that tantalizing lump under his jeans. His grand-dam seems quite happy for us, and after we've sat with her for lunch, she waves us off.

"I think the two of you have plenty of things to do that aren't hanging out with your old lady," she says to Theo, whacking him playfully on the shoulder. "Go take Celeste on a date somewhere." Her brown eyes remind me of Theo's. "Take good care of him, will you?" she asks me.

"Of course." I take his hand in mine. Maybe we don't know yet if this will be permanent, but for as long as I have him, I will. "I'll do my best," I say.

Theo gives his grand-dam a kiss on each of her cheeks, and then she waves us off.

"I think that went well," Theo says as we hop into the truck.

"I liked her. She reminds me of you."

He leans down to kiss me on the lips, and then plants another one on my forehead. "Thanks for going with me. It meant a lot."

It felt like a big step forward, and I'm giddy for the next one.

Unfortunately, Theo has to go back to work on Monday. I meet him at the door on his way out. He hugs me tight, as if he'd rather do anything else but leave me here.

"Do whatever you like," he says. "All the gardening tools are in the garage. You might even try taking the dogs out."

I'm shocked. "But that wouldn't be safe, would it?" I'd be fully vulnerable to any monster wandering around the neighborhood.

"Bug and Ramona will keep you safe." Then he kisses me on the forehead, and leaves me at the front door.

I'm disappointed to watch him pull out of the driveway, but he calls out the window that he'll be home right at five, just in time to make dinner together. Then he's gone.

I wonder what I'll do all day here alone. First, I set to taking care of the plants, picking off dead leaves, watering the roots and finding warm places where they'll get plenty of light. I draw up plans for where a garden could go, and what we should plant where given the house's east facing. The dogs keep me company, thrilled to have someone home with them all day. I set out my easel in my room, spreading some newspaper under it so paint doesn't drip onto the carpet, and start sketching out the view from my window. I do everything I can think to do, and by three I'm in a cuddle puddle on the couch with the dogs, watching trashy talk shows.

Once we get the garden going I'll have a lot more to keep me occupied, but I can't help feeling a little useless already. I can't go and run errands or get a job of my own.

Until the idea occurs to me that maybe I could find some telecommute gig, and I start searching right away. But it's tedious work to look, and I'm not really qualified for any of the jobs I find.

I'm relieved beyond measure when Theo finally gets home. I run to hug him, but he wards me off. "I smell terrible, sweetheart," he says. "We're working on a new property and I was out in the sun all day, sweating my ass off."

Except that I like the warm, spicy scent of his musk, so I hug him anyway. I want more, and more, and more.

"I don't mind," I say, burying my face between his big, soft pectorals. "I kinda like it." I more than like it, actually. It's so intoxicating I could probably put my nose in his armpit and enjoy it.

"Is that so?" Theo wraps me up in his arms and bends forward so I'm fully ensconced in him, and sighs into my hair. "Then there's plenty to go around."

Eventually he does go to take a shower, and I get to work cutting the vegetables for dinner until he joins me. His hand trails across my lower back as he passes me in the kitchen, carrying the pasta to the sink so it can drain. Feeling buoyed by his presence, I can already imagine what it'll be like to be cared for by Theo.

I hope that I can do the same for him, and be the partner he was seeking when he sent in his application.

That night we watch a movie, but Theo falls asleep partway through. His work must be exhausting, so I let him keep sleeping even when the screen turns black and it returns to the DVD menu.

"Theo?" I finally ask, running a hand down his chest. "We should go to bed now."

But his arm only curls tighter around me, and he lets out a pleased grunt as his nose nuzzles my hair. His lips travel down to my temple, then my ear, where he nibbles gently on the lobe, and now I know he's awake. A shiver spiders out from this one point of contact, and goosebumps cover my arms.

Then his mouth continues down my jaw to my neck. His breaths are coming faster, less controlled, as his lips trail over my collarbone. I'm tingling all over now, my body responding with little gasps as he explores my skin.

Suddenly Theo pauses, and leans back so he can look in my eyes. "Maybe you're right," he says. "We should go to bed." But the tone of his voice tells me he wants anything but that. There's that large shape developing inside his jeans again, and I can sense he's trying his best not to let me know how he's really feeling. Already his hand is subconsciously roaming up and down my hip, telling me what it is he actually wants.

"I guess so," I say uncertainly. "You do have to get up early for work." It's getting late, but neither of us move. My hand is frozen on his knee, only a few inches away from the lump on his leg. The fact that he wants me, that I'm causing this reaction in him, stirs a need deep in my belly. A devilish part of me wonders what would happen if I touched it. What would he do?

Theo suddenly clears his throat and stands up, disentangling from me and disturbing the dogs where they've been sleeping at our feet. "Right. I don't want to be a zombie on the job tomorrow. Doug already has the monopoly on being undead."

I'm disappointed, even though I know I shouldn't be. As much as I'd rather have spent the rest of the night curled in Theo's side, maybe running my hands over that object under his jeans, real life calls.

Once we're in our respective rooms with the lights out, I can't stop thinking about it and how much I wanted to touch it. What would Theo do with it if it were freed? I imagine other places his hands could be besides just brushing over my hip. There's a pulsing between my legs as each of these images unfurls in my mind, sending blood rushing straight down.

I had toys at the compound, but I left them tucked in a drawer, worried that Theo might go through my things and find them—not that he would ever do that, of course. Now I wish I'd brought them along because I'm throbbing just thinking about Theo's big body, his soft but calloused hands, his thick belly with the firm muscle underneath. I bet it would feel amazing under me.

That leaves one option. I peel off my clothes, and before I

get into pajamas, I turn off the light and lie back on the soft, flower-pattern comforter. When my fingers find their way down between my legs I find I'm already rather juicy, and my lower lips are thick and swollen up. I start out with my clit, just teasing it gently, but the moment my mind finds its way back to Theo's arm around me on the couch, my hand speeds up. I can easily imagine his huge body over mine, shadowing me, protecting me, his wide horns standing in stark contrast to the overhead light. Maybe it would be in my room, or maybe it would be in his—but I think he would remove my clothes slowly, taking in each new part of me as it's revealed to him. That's how Theo does everything, after all: deliberate, thoughtful, steady. I imagine his huge mouth nibbling me the way he did tonight but lower, all the way down my naked body. I gasp as more liquid seeps out of me, lubricating my hand as I rub myself faster and faster. I've never thought about anyone the way I'm thinking about Theo now, and my back arches as a quiet, delicious pleasure starts to spread up my spine.

I've had sex a few times with other humans at the compound, Rob included. But it was only ever for the sex, meant to blow off some steam and try to quench the thirst. I never felt hunger for any of my partners, not past the crushes I had as a teenager. But Theo... I want to touch him all over. I want to kiss him back the way he kissed me tonight. I want, I want, I want. I want so much that it's easy to take myself to the finish line, and then I gasp when I realize I'm dripping down onto the perfect, new comforter, and quickly hop off to go to the bathroom and clean myself up.

As I pass Theo's room, I hear a sound—a deep, low grunt, and then Theo's gasping breaths. I freeze, stopping in front of the door.

It doesn't take a rocket scientist to piece together what's happening on the other side. I take a step closer and lean my ear against the door. I feel like I'm violating his privacy by over-hearing this, but I can't stop myself. The sound of his hushed groans brings back my own roaring need. I keep listening as I reach down between my legs, and he gets closer and closer to his own finish. I imagine him with his hand wrapped around his dick, and I wonder what it looks like. I wish I could see him, his fist pumping as he gets closer, but just the sound of his low moan as he climaxes is enough to do me in.

Finally I regain my senses, and hurry on to the bathroom before he can catch me eavesdropping.

I decide that tomorrow, I have to do something about this. Now I know Theo wants me, too.

I put my pajamas on and curl up in bed, imagining he's there with me, his big body wrapped up tight around mine.

Chapter Eight

When Theo leaves for work the next morning, I boldly stand up on my toes and kiss him on the mouth. Soon he has me so close it's like he's afraid I won't be here when he gets back.

"I'll be home soon. Maybe early if we finish up the rest of this framing. Okay?" He strokes the side of my face with his thumb. "I'll bring home some extra wood and we can start putting up the boxes."

So he was serious about building a garden. I'm thrilled. "I'll mark out where they should go," I say, pretending to click a pen. "Draw up battle plans."

He looks pleased with my answer. "I can't wait to see what you grow."

Once Donald Duck has pulled out of the driveway—Theo's adorable name for the truck with its mismatched yellow hood—I busy myself with stakes, selecting a spot in the hottest part of the yard for peppers and tomato plants, then drawing out an idea for a hoop house to help them grow even faster. We could probably use leftover moulding from the site to build a trellis for peas and cucumbers, and then plant straight in the ground for onions and carrots and squash.

If we could pull this off, I might be able to grow enough food that we don't need to buy anything but tofu and dry goods.

Spending the morning on the garden plan still leaves me time to apply for jobs answering phone calls or working as a virtual assistant. Not having a job when I lived at the compound was fine because I had responsibilities there, but now I feel like I ought to contribute something.

Still, I have no luck at all. I submit a few applications for things I'm far under-qualified for and wonder if maybe I should give some more thought to online school.

Around four, I get a text from Theo saying he's on the way home. It feels like a soft blanket over my shoulders. I might actually get to live a life as normal as this.

The dogs are almost as excited as I am when he walks in the door, carrying a bag of takeout. "I know it's early for dinner," he says, leaning down to kiss me on the forehead as he kicks the door closed behind him, "but I thought you might want to spend some time on your new project while it's still light out. I brought plenty of scrap wood home from the job site. It's all out in the truck."

My heart soars. He thought about me while he was at work, and even planned a whole evening for us. I wrap my arms around him tight and squeeze, filling it with all the emotion bubbling up inside me. With an affectionate chuckle, he hugs me back, still holding the takeout bag.

Once we're done eating, we take stock of the wood available to us. Once it's all organized by size, we can decide exactly what shape of boxes to make, and Theo already has all the tools he needs in the garage. We get the first two put together, with me holding the wood in place while he drills in each hole for a dowel. Once they're assembled, I point where I want them to go according to my diagram.

"That one will be in the shade," I explain. "Perfect for growing lettuce and spinach."

"Spinach!" Theo is completely sincere in his enthusiasm for spinach. "I hope you plant a ton."

The sun is finally retreating as I show him where I think we should put the in-ground garden, which will hold all of our root vegetables, squash, and melons.

"I'll see if I can get my hands on some wire fencing," he says. "I would hate for rabbits to get in and destroy them all before they can grow."

While we finish up putting away the tools, Theo talks to me about the new building they're working on, and I tell him how I spent my day.

He wipes the sweat from his forehead as we walk inside. "I hope you're not looking for a job because you feel like you have to," he says, pouring out a glass of water for each of us. "I want to take care of you. I want you to be happy here."

"I am happy here." I wring my hands. "But I don't want to be a drain."

Theo places down his water so firmly that the glass clinks on the counter. His face is serious as he approaches me, his arm looping around my waist.

"You're anything but a drain," he says, leaning down to kiss the crown of my head. "I asked for someone to dote on, someone who would be my companion in life. I want to give you everything you want, Celeste." He looks me in the eyes, taking both of my hands in his. "Will you let me?"

To be looked at this way, with such warm sincerity, makes my chest feel like it might burst. But can I really give him all of myself yet? Can I trust him to always take care of me the way he is now?

"I need to feel useful," I say at last. "Maybe it could be fun money. Or I could buy something big with it, like a new couch."

Theo frowns and looks at the couch. "You don't like it?"

Me and my big mouth.

"Honestly..." I begin, not sure what to say that won't further offend him.

He offers me an apologetic smile. "You can be honest."

I sigh. "That couch must be twenty years old, and I basically disappear into it when I sit down." I flop onto the cushion to show him what I mean, and it swallows me up. "I'd just like to be able to touch the floor with my feet."

Rubbing his chin, Theo examines it. "You might be right. I didn't consider how much smaller you are."

He falls down onto the couch next to me, bouncing me upward and making us both giggle like kids. Then he draws me into his arms and drops his head to press his muzzle into my neck.

"We'll get a new couch," he murmurs. "I want you to feel comfortable."

"Thank you." I let him envelop me. "I already do."

The house has gotten dark as the sun sets, but neither of us moves to turn on a light. Theo runs his lips up and down my neck slowly, languidly, as if he's in no rush and simply wants to savor me. There's a tension in the air, like one of us speaking would break the spell. Tentatively I reach out with one hand and place it on his big chest. He doesn't react, so I draw it downward, finally testing out the feel of the body I've been thinking about so much. When I reach his abdomen, where the bottom hem of his tight work shirt has been pulled up to his belly button, something under his jeans jumps. I test this reaction, running my hand even closer to the hem this time, and that thick lump pressed tight against his thigh spasms again. Theo's breath hitches, and every bone in my body wants to just reach out and touch it. But is he as ready for me as I am for him?

"Theo." He freezes when I whisper his name, so I stroke his belly to show him I'd like to keep touching. "If you want me, you should tell me." Maybe if I give him an open forum, he'll take the step.

He doesn't answer right away, but he resumes kissing the side of my neck. He runs his lips up to my ear.

"I want you." Theo's voice is as soft and smooth as silk, but there's an edge of trepidation to it, too. "I really, really want you, Celeste."

Heat explodes across my body. I trace my hands down to his thigh, and then finally, I brush over the long bulge that's only gotten bigger and harder. Theo exhales sharply. His hands have grown bolder, too, and I wish there weren't any layers of fabric between us. I want to get to see him, to marvel at him and enjoy him and sample every inch of him. My need is reflected back at me when Theo looks down into my eyes, and the soft sweetness in them boils me over. I press a rough kiss to his lips, my free hand dragging upward to duck underneath his shirt. He audibly groans underneath me.

"You're so incredibly hot," I tell him, exploring his strong belly.

"Me?" He sounds surprised, as if he has no idea just how tasty he is.

"Yes, you." I peel the shirt up, and Theo eagerly helps me take it off of him. He has to carefully navigate it over his horns, and while he's occupied, I continue memorizing the shape of his hefty body, tracing the pattern of the fur on his chest and belly where the black gives way to white.

When his hands return to me again, he's more sure, more demanding. His kisses press me back against the couch, and his big fingers explore my waist. He draws away and gently tugs up the hem of my shirt, then stops to look up at me for permission. I pull it up over my arms, and then I'm just in my bra. Theo's big, wide-set eyes are half-lidded and pleased.

"You're beautiful, sweetheart," he says. His hands trail up my sides, grazing the swell of my breasts and dipping down again. He's looking at me like I'm the only other person in existence. "I can't wait to see more of you."

More? Yes, please. I want to take off every last item of clothing that stands between us and feel his big, furry body against mine.

At last he reaches around and unhooks my bra, letting the straps fall down my arms. Then his hands are on me, rubbing my nipples, cradling them between his big, thick fingers while he teases the tips with his thumbs. I'm melting into his hands, and they're holding me up as he leans down to take one of my breasts in his mouth.

"Oh, Theo," I whisper, running my hands down his soft ears while he laps me with his rough tongue, stimulating every nerve ending in my chest. I'm arching into him and he's sucking me harder, brushing just the edge of his flat teeth over each nipple. I wonder if I could come like this, with only his hands and mouth on my tits. It's not outside the realm of possibility.

Once he rises back to his full height, I try to focus on my task of teasing him through his jeans, up and down the length of him. He groans and his hips spasm, and I wonder if it feels as tight and uncomfortable inside there as it looks. Finally, I move to unbutton his pants, and he sits up sharply.

"Theo?" I ask, worried that I've moved too quickly.

"We should..." His voice is low and husky. "Maybe we should go, um, upstairs." His dark eyes lock onto mine. "Do you want to go in my room?"

Oh, do I ever. I've been dying to see the inside of his bedroom, not just because I'm curious about his decorating.

"Yes," I say. "Yes, I do."

Theo reaches underneath me and hefts me up into his arms by the waist. I squeal and wrap my legs around him so I don't fall, and he easily carries me across the living room and up the stairs, to the final door at the end of the hallway. His door.

He practically kicks it down, and the knob bounces off the wall.

This is the Theo I knew was in there.

Chapter Nine

It's the first time I've seen beyond just the doorway. Theo has a big, California King bed, which doesn't surprise me given his size. Mirrors run all along his closet doors, reflecting whatever's happening in front of them. Immediately I imagine myself there on my hands and knees, watching my reflection while Theo is behind me, and I clench around something between my legs that isn't there. I wonder if the kinky mirrors are on purpose—if he put them here for this reason. I'm getting wet just thinking about it.

Theo bends over the bed and sets me down gently on my back, letting my legs hang off the side. His jeans are still tantalizingly unbuttoned, but I stay where he's put me, waiting for what he has in mind next. He studies me for a long time, almost too long, then he crouches down at the edge of the bed between my legs. Delicately, he uses his huge fingers to take off my pants, sliding them over my bare feet and tossing them aside. Now only my underwear hides me from him.

"Yours now," I say, keeping my gaze riveted on him. "I want to see you, too."

A smile flashes across Theo's face, and it's almost mischievous. I like bedroom Theo. He unzips his jeans and pushes them off his hips, pulling his tail out through the slot at the back. Then he kicks them off and he's just in his boxer-briefs, which fit perfectly around his toned ass and impressively large package.

There it is—just what I've been waiting for. He's straining hard at his underwear, and now I need nothing more than to see him without them, but he shakes his head when I reach towards him.

"Stay there, sweetheart," he says firmly, and I'm surprised. But I find that I like him telling me what to do. It feels safe, like whatever he says is for my own good.

He crouches over me on the bed and explores me with his hands, from my collar down to the mound of my pelvis. He slides his fingers between my legs, and they reflexively part for him. With long, smooth strokes, he teases me over the gusset of my underwear, and I can feel how damp I'm making them.

Theo is breathing harder, his nostrils flared and those wide-set eyes hooded. I reach down and peel off my underwear, tired of this one more thing keeping us apart. His lips pull up on one side of his muzzle.

"In a rush?" he asks. "We have all night."

The way he says it, I imagine hours of my huge minotaur taking me in front of those mirrors. That's what I need, right now.

"I want to feel your hands on me," I say. "I've... I've wanted it for a while now."

His smile widens, and obediently his fingers wind back down my belly and through the small patch of hair there. "Then I'd love to give it to you." He drops forward onto one elbow, and with our faces so close together, he devours my lips in his just as his hand reaches my warm, wet center.

Yes, this is what I was after. He circles my outer lips with the pad of his finger, as if he's just getting to know me, and I gasp. Then he ducks under the hood and presses a ghost of a touch on my clit, which earns a moan. His hands feel like starlight.

"Sensitive," he says into my ear. "So sensitive." Again he teases my clit and again I tremble, and he repeats the motion until I'm arching into his stiff belly. But I want more. I want his fingers inside me. I want *him* inside me.

Unfortunately, Theo takes his time, stroking again and again until my small slit is weeping with my arousal.

"There we are, sweetheart," he says, running his tongue over the shell of my ear. "You're so, so wet for me."

Whatever this side of Theo this is, who talks dirty and sweet at the same time, I like it. I crave it. He reaches down and his finger gently presses inside, and I'm surprised by how large he is, how much my muscles have to relax just to let it in.

"So small." Theo sinks his finger in deeper and it feels so good, like an appetizer before an amazing meal. It's just a hint of what's to come. "I don't know if I'll fit inside you."

Those words are like a bolt of lightning from my heart straight down to where his finger is filling me up. I gasp and clench, imagining how he would feel.

"I'm sure you will," I manage between gasps.

But Theo just shakes his head. He gently withdraws his finger from me, and I let out a mewl of disappointment.

"I'll be back for you," he says, standing up again. He snags the band of his boxer briefs and pulls them down over his cock, and it suddenly springs free. It's even bigger than I thought it was by the outline under his jeans. It's black and thick and full with blood, and sizable veins spider across the length of it. A huge, dark sac hangs down below. My mouth is dry. He's as big as my forearm, and I'm instantly enamored.

"I want it, Theo. Please." I'm already so riled up and so wet for him.

He peels his underwear down over his hooves and tosses them aside. "I like to hear that." Crouching over me, he gently kisses me on the lips. "But you're not ready for me. Not yet."

"Not yet?" I've never been more ready than I am now.

He nods. "We just have to get you ready." Then his voice drops low, and I can feel that enormous cock against my thigh. "Stretch you out a little so you can fit me."

My eyebrows go straight up. "What does that mean?"

Lowering his body to mine so I can feel his warmth and sense the heft of him, he says, "I'll show you, if you'll let me."

I look into Theo's eyes. Am I ready to put all my faith in him? Maybe we don't know each other that well yet, but I feel like I understand him. He won't lead me wrong.

"Okay," I say.

With a nod and a sweet smile, Theo tugs me to the edge of the bed so he can spread my legs apart even further. Then he kneels down, and I realize what he's going to do.

The sensation of his rough tongue over my pussy instantly sets my skin ablaze. I moan and grip one of his horns as he traces my outer lips. Then he moves inward, and I'm holding on with both hands like I'm riding a motorcycle. Finally he reaches my clit, circling it tighter and tighter until I'm whining for more, lost to the feel of him.

Once again he slides a finger inside me, and then another. Oh, those fingers are so big. It takes my body a moment to adjust, but soon he's licking me and pumping me, urging me on toward that bright point at the end of the tunnel.

That's when his hand pauses, and I hear him pull open the drawer of his bedside table. He removes something from it, and when I open my eyes, he has a blue dildo in his hands. It's not nearly as big as he is, still fully erect for me. In fact, it's barely a fraction of his size.

"This is step one," Theo says, showing me the toy. *Step one?* I wonder how many steps there are. A bottle of lube follows, and he coats the head of the dildo with it. Then he kneels down in front of the bed so he's peering up at me over my curls. "Can I put this inside you?"

Hot embarrassment rushes into my face. Sure, I've used one on myself, but never with a partner.

I think with Theo, though, I would enjoy it. So finally I say, "Yes."

I watch with wide eyes as he brings the tip down between my legs, and resumes licking me. It's perfect. Then I feel the gentle prod of the dildo.

"Oh!" The head wiggles around, and it's cold against my skin. I shiver a little as the lube spreads all around me, and slowly, the head slips inside. I'm tighter than I anticipated, but Theo takes his time, and I'm overcome by the flicking of his tongue over me while the dildo retreats, then pushes through once more. Soon I'm writhing underneath him, my body taken over by tremors as he works it slowly inside me, just dipping it in as far as it will go and withdrawing it, softening me, loosening me up. He takes his time, convincing each layer of me to relax and spread for it.

"There we are," he says in that low, quiet rumble of his. "Let it all in." He laves that wide, textured tongue over my clit while he opens me wider and wider. "You're so beautiful, Celeste," he murmurs against me. "I can't wait until I can have you."

"I want you, Theo," I moan as he buries the dildo ever deeper.

"I want you, too," he says between licks.

And then, suddenly, it's all the way inside. I cry out as I

tangle my hands in Theo's hair, and I think my body might just combust. He starts to pump the dildo inside me, and soon it's slicking in and out so fast my hips are bucking against it. I can't control the stream of sounds coming out of my mouth.

"Very good," Theo says, wiping his lips with one arm as he stands up. Still fucking me with the dildo, he reaches down to his own huge cock and strokes it with his other hand, watching me with half-lidded eyes as I thrash and moan.

"Am I..." I cut myself off with a gasp when the dildo reaches even deeper. "Am I ready yet?"

"No, sweetheart." He pumps himself faster, matching the tempo of the dildo. Pre-come drips from the tip of his huge cock, and he smears it around himself before continuing. "Not yet." His movements speed up until he's pounding into me and into his hand at the same time, as if he's imagining himself in the dildo's place just like I am. Watching him touch himself brings me closer and closer to the edge until all I want is to break. I'm crying out and my hips are snapping up in rhythm with his, my body begging for release. I can see myself in the mirrors, writhing while Theo stands over me, running his hand up and down his incredible cock as he gazes down at me. Now I understand why they're here.

The dildo strikes deep inside me once more and then I'm there, finally at the end of the dark tunnel and racing out into the light. It takes over me and I cry out, "Theo! Yes!" as wave after wave washes over me.

In the blinding brightness, I hear Theo grunt, and then moan as he reaches the sky with me. A powerful stream of white shoots out of him, lancing through the air to land on my belly. He squeezes himself a few more times, his shoulders curled with the sheer force of his orgasm, and even more of his come drips onto my thigh. We're both panting, and the sheen of sweat covering my forehead slides down into my eyes as I sit up to look at him. Slowly, Theo removes the dildo, then sets it on the bedside table and reaches into the drawer for a box of kleenexes.

"You did so well, sweetheart." He cleans me, softly gathering up all his fluid and mine, and then tosses the tissues in the trash.

"I don't know what I did, though," I say. He lies down next to me with a chuckle, his huge weight sinking into the soft bed. I curl into his warmth, into the velvety fur covering his chest.

"You took the toy wonderfully," he says, petting my hair and nuzzling my head with his big muzzle. "When you're used to it, we'll try the bigger toy, and see how you accept that."

I quiver at the thought of another dildo, even broader than this one, filling me up. "And that's so you can fit inside me?" I ask tentatively.

"Yes. This way you'll be ready to take me, and it will feel good." He embraces me with his big arms and hands, wrapping me up tight. "So, so good."

It feels right to lie here, surrounded by him—righter than anything I've felt in my life. It's easy to fall asleep like that, curled into his soft side, using his big forearm for a pillow.

Nothing can touch me here.

Chapter Ten

The next morning, I'm certain that I'll get addicted to waking up next to Theo. He has one arm slung across his face to hide his eyes from the morning sun coming in the window, the other lying under my neck like a pillow. My shoulders feel a little sore, but it was worth it to sleep curled up in his side, drinking in the warm, familiar smell of him.

When he finally opens his eyes, his big muzzle is overtaken by a smile. It's such a lovely, soft smile that I feel like I might just turn into a gelatinous puddle here in the bed. He rolls me up with his arm and presses a fierce kiss to my forehead.

At last, we get up, because Theo has to get to work—but he insists on making breakfast first.

"Did you like it?" he asks, coming to stand behind me at the table. He gently rubs my shoulders. "What we did last night?"

Instantly I'm blushing. "Yeah, I did. A lot." Getting naked with Theo was one of the best things to ever happen to me.

"Good." His neck is so long he has no trouble leaning down and kissing my crown from his full height. "Then we'll do some more."

I thought he might be more shy when it comes to talking about sex, but it just seems to naturally meld with his personality. He talks about it the same way he talks about what we're going to eat for dinner, and it's sexy and comforting, like what we're doing is exactly how things should be.

But I do have something else on my mind, a question I'm not sure I want to know the answer to, but I need to ask.

"Theo..." I say, hesitating.

He pauses while taking my plate to the dishwasher. "Yes?"

"Those toys." I clear my throat, keeping my eyes on the table. I try to push down the jealousy rising in my chest just at the thought of what I'm about to ask. "Did you already have them? From... from someone else?"

His eyes go as wide as saucers, and his mouth falls slightly open.

"Oh, sweetheart." Theo drops the plate into the sink, then pulls me up out of the chair and into his arms. "No, of course not. I got them, um, right before you moved in." He starts stumbling over his words. "But please don't think I came into this with an expectation we would have sex. I just... I thought I should be prepared, in case you wanted that, too."

Relief floods through me. I reach up, wrap my arms around him, and pull him down to kiss me. He relaxes into me, returning it tenfold.

"I've wanted to climb you like a tree since you first kissed me," I say. "In fact, I've been hoping you'd put the moves on me for days now."

His eyebrows rise. "You have?"

It makes me feel like a bit of a horn dog, but while we're being honest with each other... "Oh yeah. Actually, I heard you in your room the other night, and, um," I swallow hard. I can't believe I'm admitting this. "It was so hot. I, uh, even touched myself listening to you."

Theo simply gapes at me. Then he laughs, and it's a big, booming laugh. He draws me as tight against him as he possibly can and rubs the side of my face with his nose.

"You're so wonderful, Celeste," he says. "I can't believe I was that loud."

"Were you thinking about me?" I ask, batting my eyelashes.

He coughs. "Of course. You're super hot, and you smell so good when we make out... I couldn't help it."

I giggle. "Good." I push him away. "You'd better get going so you aren't late."

On his way out the door, Theo pauses to run a hand down my back, then cups my ass in a way that's surprisingly bold.

"Can't wait to see you later," he whispers in my ear. A shock of thrill rushes down my spine, and then he heads off for work, leaving me on the front step with a warm tingle between my legs.

"You have to tell me *everything*," says Maddie. She's quite literally bouncing on her bed, where I'm sure her laptop is perched somewhere precarious. "I can't believe you and Theo are having sex already!"

"Well, yes and no," I say. "We haven't done any, uh—you know, *penetration*. He says I'm not, um..." I've never had to talk to someone about my sex life because I've never had one before.

"You're not what, Celeste? Spit it out."

"He's really big, okay?" I cover my face, hoping it will mask my embarrassment. "So we have to work up to it. I guess."

But Maddie just nods along. "Yes, yes, of course." She smiles through the computer screen. "Good. Egorr and I had the same problem." I guess that shouldn't surprise me given his size. He might be as tall as Theo or taller, before the horns. "Neither of us really understood what we were getting into." She cringes, and so do I.

"Yikes."

"Theo sounds like a good match for you." She strokes her chin thoughtfully. "Maybe we should try to get together or something? I'd like to meet him."

I guess we do live near the same city now. "You're saying, like, a double date?" I ask. Another one of those fun things I never got to do when I lived in New Eden.

"Yeah, exactly! A double date."

We make some plans and run them past Theo and Egorr. They both eagerly agree.

It's a date.

I didn't think our first argument would be over pizza.

"Excuse me? You want what?" I ask Theo, incredulous.

He frowns. "You don't like green olives?"

I slap down the menu and drop my head into my hands. "The green olives aren't the problem. It's the fact you want green olives *and* pineapple. On the same pizza!"

The waitress, a big moth-woman with fluffy antennae, carefully avoids our table.

"It's delicious," Theo says, flashing me a grin. "Don't knock it 'til you try it."

Ever since that night, I feel like I've been seeing more and more of this Theo—the one who picked me up and carried me to the truck because I was too full to walk. The one who makes jokes, who calls me *sweetheart* and tells me what to do. It feels safe and easy to be around that Theo.

Except for the fact he doesn't know how to eat pizza.

Finally we agree on a laundry list of toppings, and decide to divide the pizza in half, even though he'll easily eat three-quarters of it.

The shop door opens with a jingle of bells, and Maddie steps inside with a lumbering green giant right behind her. Overwhelmed by the sight of her again, I leap out of the seat and run to hug her. A few of the monsters sitting at the bar turn to stare at me.

"Aw, I'm happy to see you, too," Maddie says, patting my back. She steps aside, revealing Egorr's lower half. I have to tilt my head to look up at him just like I do with Theo. "Egorr, this is Celeste."

"Hello," Egorr's big voice booms. His huge tusks reach past his eyes as he smiles. "Maddie talks about you a lot."

We shake hands, and his are even bigger than Theo's. Speaking of which—he's joined us now, so I do the same introduction with Maddie. A big, pleased smile takes over her face as Theo shakes her hand.

"I'm really glad we're doing this," Theo says. He stands up straight again and strokes my shoulder. "Now you get to have some friend time, and I get to meet the person most important to you."

Maddie is simply swooning. "I didn't know I meant that much to you, Celeste," she teases, winking at me. "It's good to meet you too, Theo. I've heard a lot about you." She surveys him up and down, utterly objectifying him. "She didn't say how hot you are, though."

I'm trapped between saying *I did tell you!* and *He's mine!* Neither of which are very appropriate right now.

Theo just scratches the back of his head and smiles nervously, not saying anything in response. I remember how shy he was with me when we first met, and I know I need to rescue him.

"Hey, Maddie," I say, gesturing to our table. "Let's sit down so we can all order together, huh?" Theo shoots me a grateful look as I guide Maddie and Egorr into their seat at the booth across from us.

Egorr looks over the menu once, then says, "One cheese pizza and one pepperoni." Maddie doesn't look at it at all.

"Two whole pizzas?" I ask.

"We order pizza out a lot at home," Egorr says with a little bit of shame. "We always get the same thing. One cheese, one pepperoni. I eat most of it, she eats two pieces of each."

It's cute that they already have such a steady rhythm to their lives. I wonder if someday Theo and I will be able to order for each other, too.

Once we've gotten the moth waitress's attention and told her what we want, Maddie immediately starts talking. I'm glad she's here, frankly, because Egorr seems about as talkative as Theo in a group setting—which is not at all.

"We're thinking of getting a cat," Maddie's saying. "Egorr doesn't want me being at home alone all day, even though I have plenty of online friends." She taps the table. "I'm excited. I've never had a pet before."

"Do you know what you want to name it?" Theo asks, and I look at him with surprise. There's a look of concentration on his face, like he's putting in a concerted effort into making conversation.

Maddie grins widely. "I was going to decide when we got it, you know, to maybe choose something based on its personality... But I've also always wanted a pet named Baby. I just think it would be cute, you know?" She sighs a little. "Especially since we can't ever, you know." She gestures at Egorr.

Oh, right. Having any real babies is out of the picture for them, too. I glance out of the corner of my eye at Theo. If we decided to get married after the trial, the same would be true for us. I wonder if that bothers him. It's not like his species is endangered the way mine is. He has the opportunity, if he wants, to have children. *Calves?* I'm not sure.

"That's a super cute name," I say. "You should name your cat that, for sure."

Maddie beams at me. It's wonderful to see her in person again. Those Zoom calls don't compare at all to the real article.

We make pleasant conversation after that, mostly Maddie and I talking while Egorr and Theo listen. I ask about Egorr's work, and he's proud to announce he's now working from home two days a week so he can spend more time with Maddie. He got special permission from his boss, having a human companion and all.

"All my coworkers are jealous," he says with a big laugh.

Wow. He got a perk like that just because he's married to a human? "Are we really that, um, desirable for monsters?" I ask.

Both Egorr and Theo turn to me like I've just spoken in another language. Egorr cocks an eyebrow, and Theo's mouth falls slightly open. Maddie just laughs.

"You have no idea, huh?" She snorts. "Theo's probably getting ribbed about it all day on the worksite."

Theo gives a nervous chuckle. "Yeah. I guess so."

"Why?" I ask, glancing between Theo and Maddie. "What's so appealing about us?"

"Well," Egorr says, shoulders tensing, "humans are cute. And small. And..."

Maddie leans forward conspiratorially. "They want to fuck us," she whispers.

Theo runs a hand down his nose, and if he could blush, his face would probably be neon red.

"Oh." I rub my own warm cheeks. "I guess that makes sense."

Luckily, Maddie's already moved on. "But you can't really work from home, can you?" she says to Theo.

Sheepishly, he shakes his head. "Not really, no. I've thought about cutting down my hours—"

I gasp. "No way. You shouldn't take time off of work just so you can be at home with me more."

"But..." Theo begins.

Maddie mock-gasps. "Is this your first marital fight?"

"Stop being an instigator," I chide her, and she laughs. Even though Theo and I aren't fully married, I liked the way it sounded.

Theo seems to understand then that she's kidding, and exhales a breath of relief. My hand finds its way into his lap, and he quickly takes it in his big fingers.

"Anyway," Maddie says, "it's not like I'm always stuck at home. I've started going to the grocery store sometimes."

My throat clamps shut. "What? You're going out of the house by yourself?"

"Just to the store." She smiles at Egorr, who doesn't look nearly as thrilled about it. "I had to do a lot of convincing, though."

"Maddie." I'm serious as I say it. "That's not a good idea."

"Why not?" She huffs. "It's a public place. And it's only for a few minutes."

"All it takes is a few minutes!" How can she be so thought-less? Immediately I imagine Maddie, just a husk of herself after a vampire has gotten hold of her in the chip aisle while no one was looking.

"Hey, calm down," Maddie says. "It's fine. I've gone twice now and no big deal, right, Egorr?"

He just nods. There's really no fighting Maddie once she's decided on something, but I'm terrified for her.

Under the table, Theo squeezes my hand, and it's just enough to bring me back down to earth. I shoot him a grateful look.

Finally, our pizza arrives, but I can't stop thinking about Maddie driving alone to the store and not coming back.

Chapter Eleven

When we head home after dinner, I think Theo senses my dark mood, because we don't talk much on the drive. He runs a hand along my thigh, though, to let me know he's there if I want to discuss whatever is bothering me.

I'm not sure how I got so lucky. I'm glad I took a chance on him. But I'm still lost in my thoughts even as we pull into the driveway.

"We're here," Theo says.

I jolt at the sound of his voice. He brushes some hair behind my ear and asks, "Let me know if I can help, okay?"

Instead of answering, I leap across the seat and wrap my arms around his neck. I want the security he makes me feel when we're together. I want the smooth comfort of his fur. I want to think of anything but the outside world.

"I had a lovely time," I say into his shoulder. "But I'm scared for her, Theo."

He holds me gently, rubbing small circles on my back. "I

know, sweetheart." He sighs. "Egorr has got to worry while he's at work. I would."

"I'd never make you worry like that." I tell him. "Never."

His hand slows.

"Celeste." Theo leans back so he can look into my eyes. "It's fine if I have to worry sometimes, you know. I'd way rather worry about you a little so you can live a full life, then see you always marooned in the house and afraid of going out on your own."

"But if I went without you..." My arms prickle with goosebumps. "Anything could happen."

"I'm not saying you need to go to the grocery store like Maddie," Theo says, wrapping my hand up in his. "But I don't want you to live afraid, either. It's a good neighborhood. There's a nice yeti who lives across the street, and I know he would help look out for you."

I try to let my shoulders relax. He's right. He lives in a cozy, quiet area. The likelihood of running into a monster that wants to devour me *is* rather small.

"All right," I say eventually. "You're right. You can't be with me all the time, but sometimes I should still leave the house, huh?"

He grins and kisses my forehead. "Don't want you to become a shut-in."

At last we get out of the truck, and I'm glad to see the dogs when they jump all over me, Theo telling them—rather pointlessly—to stay down.

It's already getting late, and I know Theo has to work early, but I don't want to go back to my own bed alone. However, that doesn't seem to be a question in his mind, because he takes my hand and leads me up the stairs.

"Do you want to get your toothbrush?" he asks, pausing in front of my door. "And move it into my, um, bathroom?"

Does this mean he's inviting me to stay in his room on a more permanent basis?

"Yes!" I have to work hard not to jump up in the air. "I mean, I'd love that."

His smile is wide and giddy, too. I rush into my bathroom, grab my electric brush and its charger, and follow Theo into his room.

It's both comforting and surreal to stand in the mirror next to him while we brush our teeth. His free hand trails over the small of my back, then around my hip. He pulls me in closer and watches me in the mirror with those wide, brown eyes. I can't help but look back into them, and I think I could stare into Theo's eyes forever.

He sure likes big mirrors, and I think I know why.

When we're done, he leads me to the bed and pulls the blankets back, ushering me in. Then we're curled up together, his thick arms wrapping me up tight as he kisses the crown of my head. He lets out a satisfied huff.

But I'm growing warm under my pajamas at the way we're touching, bodies pressed so close together. I can feel all of his shape against me and I love it, every swell of his chest and belly, the rippling muscle in his shoulders and arms. I wish there were fewer clothes between us, that I wasn't so small that Theo could fit inside me, because now that's all I want.

I try and try to fall asleep, but if anything, I'm buzzing with energy being so close to him, enveloped by the smell of him.

"Celeste?" Theo asks after a while, as if sensing I can't sleep.

"Yes?"

"Would it help if I did that to you again?" He drops his head down lower so his lips are next to my ear. "If I made you come around that dildo?"

Such a forward overture seems unlike him. I really like

bedroom Theo. It's as if he knows just what I want, just what I need.

"Oh, yes," I answer right away.

Despite the hour, Theo takes his time, peeling my clothes off slowly, attending to each of my nipples, covering me completely with his palms. Starting with just his fingers, he teases only the edges of my soft lower lips. Then he licks me and licks me, preparing me, getting me soaked and needy for what will come next. When he pulls out his cock, all I want is *that*, but I know I have to wait.

This time Theo guides me onto my belly, then pulls my rear up into the air. I've never been so exposed before, but I can see Theo's look of pure lust in the mirrors as he slides the blue dildo into me from behind.

It fits much easier this time, and I gasp and clench and moan as Theo strokes it in and out, pumping himself in the same rhythm. I'm mesmerized by the sight of us reflected back in the mirrors, me taking the dildo while Theo kneels down beside me, come already dribbling from the tip of his huge cock.

When he brings me to the edge, it doesn't take much for me to tip over and burst, and it feels like a bomb going off in my head. My orgasm only continues while Theo thrusts the dildo harder, his own voice climbing steadily upward, and liquid trickles down my leg. I've never orgasmed that hard in my life. Soon he's there, too, and lets out a deep low as he unleashes a powerful stream of white.

Panting, Theo flops down beside me on the bed.

"Wow," he says. He runs a hand down the side of my face. "You're so damn gorgeous. I couldn't stop looking at you as you were taking the toy." He glances down at the bedding, now complete with a streak of come across it. "Guess I'd better wash all this."

He pulls me in close and then buries us under the covers, and I think I could fall asleep like this every night.

The next day, I spend the morning making a list of which plants we need from the nursery. We'll have to make a big trip to get everything, and just the idea of seeing a greenhouse in person is exciting. Next year, we'll start the seeds ourselves indoors, and I know exactly the place they would go by the window upstairs.

Maybe I'm getting ahead of myself. Sure, we've done some pretty intimate things. But that doesn't mean Theo's going to ask me to marry him permanently. Our bodies are still getting to know each other just the way we are.

The idea of him not choosing me turns my stomach sour.

I do some job hunting, but I don't have much of a resume outside of college courses I took online. Feeling discouraged, I decide to be a little brave and go outside, like Theo suggested. It's not far to the park, and I know the dogs would like to get out. It's like he said—I can't stay marooned in the house forever. It's not healthy, and living in fear of the outside world isn't good for me in the long run. I need to take the leap, just like I did when I moved in with Theo.

Shoulders squared, I grab the leashes and take Bug and Ramona out the front door, hoping maybe I'll get some inspiration to paint.

It's a calm, peaceful walk, with a fresh breeze blowing through the neighborhood trees. The houses are quiet, and I don't run into anyone as the dogs drag me down the street. It's lovely to be outside, like Theo predicted, and I feel some of the tension from my fruitless search draining out of me.

There's no one else around when we reach the little park

with the gazebo picnic area. I brought two balls, one for each dog.

"Bug!" I call out as he runs off after a rabbit that darted into the bushes. "Bug, come back!" I'm so involved that I don't notice the shadow behind me until it's too late.

Long strips of cloth wrap around my wrist. Before I can pry them off, they jerk me back. More cloth winds around my other arm, and I let out a scream. But my attacker is stronger and has many more limbs to work with. The cloth spins me around and drags me close, so now I can see who's gotten hold of me.

A mummy. It's wrapped up entirely in layers of browned, filthy cloth, with only a few inches of face and skin exposed. Underneath the wrappings, the skin is rotted, the eyeballs fully exposed. The mouth opens wide to reveal only a few mottled teeth. I scream again, hoping that in such a public place, maybe someone will see me and help me.

This is why I'm not supposed to go out alone. Why we live on the protected preserve, why Theo keeps me so close to him.

"Bug!" I call out. "Ramona!"

A wicked grin spreads across the mummy's face. It leans closer to me, those broken teeth chomping at air. The smell is rancid.

"No one to help you," it growls, then a rotted tongue slips out to lick my face. I'm tearing at the cloth but the mummy's bindings have a mind of their own. They wrap around my legs, my waist, my throat.

In my peripheral vision, I see a blurry shape leap past me. With a feral bark one of the dogs barrels into the mummy, taking it by surprise, and some of the fabric wrapped around me loosens. It's Ramona, and she's tearing at the mummy's legs, distracting it just long enough for me to start unwinding the cloth. A moment later Bug joins her, lunging at the mummy's side and tearing out chunks of its body.

When I've removed the last wrapping, I tumble backward onto the ground. The dogs are snarling and growling as they push the mummy back. It flails its arms, and I wonder if perhaps it's afraid of them. Finally it turns around and runs, Ramona chasing after it.

"Ramona!" I call out. I can't lose Theo's dog on top of everything else. "Come back!" Reluctantly she gives up, and returns to me to lick my face. I'm shaking all over, my breaths coming in short, uneven bursts.

I almost died. I would have died, if they hadn't been here. I've been so foolish to think that living in the suburbs with Theo meant that I was safe.

Quickly, I gather up the dogs' leashes and we jog back home as fast as we can. I just hope I won't run into anyone else on the way while angry tears trickle down my cheeks.

"You're such good dogs," I tell them when we finally get home, falling into the grass in the front yard to pet their soft, wonderful heads. "Such good dogs."

I'm still trembling with adrenaline when Theo gets home that night. I told him what happened over text message, so the moment he walks in the door he's gathering me up into his arms and cradling me tight against him.

"I'm so glad you're all right." He smooths down my hair, then rubs my back, and I think he's comforting himself as much as he is me.

"Just a little rug burn," I say, though I don't feel nearly as nonplussed as I sound. Theo looks over my arms, where the mummy's wrappings left red marks on my skin. He curses under his breath and retrieves some cream from the bathroom. It soothes the burning as he rubs it in.

"I'm so sorry, sweetheart," Theo says, gathering my hands up in his. "That shouldn't have happened to you. This is my fault. I'm the one who told you—"

"No. I'm the one who shouldn't have gone out." I pitch forward on the couch. "I just didn't think that at the park..."

"Shh." Theo kisses the top of my head. "You didn't do anything wrong. You only wanted some fresh air."

"I'm so glad the dogs were with me. If they weren't..." I feel the tears building up behind my eyes now that he's here. It reminds me of the movies, when I cried next to him in the darkness. Knowing he's with me is the safety net I need to finally break down.

Theo just pulls me into his big, safe arms, murmuring gentle things into my ear as I sob. I know that I'd be dead without Bug and Ramona, and it pierces through all of the wonderful softness I've been bathing in since I moved in.

Theo heats up some frozen Chinese food that night because neither of us has the energy to cook. We watch a long movie, and I don't realize I've fallen asleep until someone is carrying me up the stairs. I can tell by the smell that it's Theo's bedroom again and I'm glad that I'm there, someplace safe, someplace where nothing can touch me.

Chapter Twelve

"I'm taking the day off today," Theo says the next morning.

I glance up from my toast and eggs. "Why?"

"I just felt like after yesterday..." He sighs. "I want to spend some time with you. Take your mind off of things."

As delightful as that sounds, I wave him off. "I'm fine, really. You should go to work. I'll stay inside today."

I'm learning that Theo can be stubborn sometimes—like a bull, you might say. He scratches the back of his head. "I've already called in."

I feel bad that he's losing a day's wages just because I had an unfortunate run-in yesterday. "You didn't have to do that."

"I know," he says. "But I wanted to. They don't even need me today." He gets out of his chair and swipes my plate, taking it to the sink. "Do you want to go out, or stay in?"

When he says *stay in*, immediately my mind jumps to when he stroked that enormous cock in front of me, taunting me with something I can't have yet, thrilling me for what's to come.

"Stay in," I say without hesitating. I want the next step, the stage two. I want that big, wide, rough tongue between my legs again. And it will certainly take my mind off of what happened yesterday.

I enjoy the way Theo's eyes crinkle, like he knows exactly what I'm thinking.

We spend the morning working on the garden to the tune of some heavy metal playing on his handheld speaker. Now that the boxes are built, it's time to get some compost for them. Together we get into Donald Duck and head off for the landfill.

I start shoveling compost into the truck bed, but I barely make a dent. Theo, on the other hand, hefts in a snow-shovel full of compost with every breath, working like a machine until the truck bed is almost full. We're both covered in dirt from head to toe, but that doesn't stop Theo from kissing me before I hop in the passenger side of the truck.

It's time to unload it when we get home, and Theo hauls wheelbarrow after wheelbarrow of compost into the garden beds, until they're all full. We supplement the soil for the in-ground garden, too, and by the end I'm dripping all over with sweat, even though Theo did most of the hard work. He looks barely fazed by it. This is what he does all day, after all—and he's doing it again on his day off.

"We should call it," I say. It's early afternoon now, and I want more than anything to go upstairs again and take off my clothes on Theo's bed.

"All right." We survey our work together, and he nods in satisfaction. "It's looking really good. I think we're ready to go pick up some plants."

I still can't believe he did all this for me, not even knowing whether I'll choose to stay or not. He's invested so much in my happiness, and it makes my chest swell with affection.

"Thank you." I throw my arms around him, and Theo hugs me back so tight he lifts me up off the ground.

"Of course, sweetheart." He kisses me square on the lips. "Your garden's going to be the talk of the whole neighborhood."

I'm about to go into the bathroom to clean up when Theo calls my name from his room.

"I was just going to take a shower," I say, gesturing at the grime that coats my entire body, even underneath my fingernails.

Theo shifts nervously from one foot to the other. "Would you like to, um, shower with me?"

Oh, do I ever. "Yes." I grab his hand in mine and squeeze it. "Yes please."

Theo leads me by the hand into his bathroom, and then to the big shower with a glass door and removable shower head. I wonder what mischievous, sexy things we could do with that shower head.

I hope it won't be long before Theo decides I'm ready for him, because I'm aching for it. I want him to take me in the shower, my back up against the tiles and my legs wrapped around his waist while the hot water slides down our bodies. And that's just one of many ways I'd like to have him.

Once we're under the stream, Theo sets to cleaning me off. He takes a soft loofah and covers it in bubbly soap, then starts to scrub me, swishing the loofah down my chest, around my breasts, to my legs. He kneels down in front of me to clean between my thighs, and when he returns to standing in front of me, his huge cock is erect and swollen. But he ignores it, turning me around so he can continue scrubbing me, down to my ass, where he carefully runs the loofah between my cheeks. I don't realize I'm letting out soft moans until Theo presses his body to my back and whispers, "Do you like that?"

I nod rapidly as his cock rubs against my butt. "Oh, yes."

It's my turn now. I take the loofah from his hand and spin around so I can get a clear view of him. The white fur on his chest is brown with dirt, so I start there, working my way from his collar down to his hips. Feeling adventurous, I keep going, drawing the loofah all the way to his groin.

Theo lets out a heavy breath, but doesn't stop me as I lather the soap in my palm and gently spread it along the surface of his cock. His hips twitch as I reach his wide, pink head, and run my soapy hands over it. The more his breath speeds up, the bolder I get, and I abandon the loofah as I wrap both hands around him. At this he groans, and braces one hand on the wall to support himself. All the muscles in his abdomen flex as I stroke him up and down along his massive length. I see why he needs to get me ready for him—now that I'm up this close, I can't imagine how it will fit inside me.

His breathing comes harder as I increase my pace. I love watching his eyes fall closed, his huge muzzle tilting back and his mouth falling open while I pleasure him. Time to explore a little bit more. While I continue squeezing and pumping him, my single hand only fitting halfway around his girth, I venture down beneath to where that furry sac hangs between his legs. It's heavy when I take it into my palms and Theo grunts, his cock spasming in my hand.

"Do you like this?" I ask, gently massaging each huge testicle.

"It's incredible." Theo leans his forehead against the tile

wall, the hot water streaming down his big body in rivulets. "You're amazing."

Good. If he likes it, then I'll give him even more.

When I've got the soap washed off of him, I kneel down and Theo asks, "Celeste?" But I don't answer because I already have my mouth on him, my lips wrapping around his soft head. Theo gasps and I hear his horns clank against the wall. "Oh, sweetheart," he groans as I twist my lips around him, lapping at the small slit in the middle of the head with my tongue. I can't even dream of taking all of him into my mouth, but there's still plenty I can do with it. I drag my lips down the side of his cock, licking at every possible intersection until Theo is panting above me, his hands clenched into fists and his hips bucking against my mouth.

"I'm going to come," Theo grunts, and I can already feel him swelling even further, his sac tightening up against his body. So I lick him harder, faster, using both hands to pump him eagerly. His hips convulse as he jams his cock into my mouth, as little as it will go, and he roars as a stream of hot liquid hits my tongue. I drink up as much as I can, relishing the sweet, salty taste of him, until I can't take any more and it starts to drip down my lips. I pump once, twice more, and Theo pitches forward like his legs might give out.

After a few panting breaths, he gazes down at me with a warm affection in his eyes. "Damn," he says breathlessly. "That was... wow. My mind is blown."

"Good." I feel a big, dumb grin bloom on my face. "Then I'll make sure to do it again."

After cleaning off my mouth, I stand back up and retrieve the loofah. Theo watches me curiously as I continue scrubbing all of his soft, black fur.

"You're still dirty," I remind him. "Have to finish what I started." I pay special attention when I reach his full, carved ass, and he inhales sharply when I push his tail out of the way and run the loofah between his cheeks, just like he did to me. Theo has brought out so many things in me I never knew about, things I never imagined for myself. Now I want to explore him everywhere, to know him all over.

Finally the hot water runs out, which is fine because my body is plenty hot without it. Theo towels me off, wrapping his huge hands around my breasts and teasing my nipples. Once we're all dry, he picks me up and carries me back to the bedroom, tossing me onto the bed with enthusiasm. I like seeing his hunger this way, and knowing that I bring it out of my shy minotaur. He drops down on his hands over me with a thirsty look in his eyes.

First he kisses me, then works his way down my body until he's between my legs again.

"I'm going to get you so wet," he says, lifting my ass up with one big, plate-sized hand. "The toy will fit inside you like a dream."

Just imagining it makes me moan, and Theo chuckles as he starts to lap me up with that broad, rough tongue. True to his word, it isn't long before his saliva and my juices have left me thoroughly slick, and that's when he reaches into the top drawer of the bedside table.

He starts out with the blue dildo again, and this time, it only takes a little work for him to slide it in. I gasp and moan as he pumps it inside of me, playing with my clit as he works it deeper and deeper, drawing pure ecstasy out of me like taffy. When I finally come around it, I come hard. Theo slows down his assault as my body clamps down tight, almost trapping it in place. When he withdraws the dildo, he's panting with his arousal, too.

"You're so gorgeous, sweetheart," he says, giving me a big, deep kiss. "You took that so well, I think it's time to graduate."

"Graduate?" I ask, sitting up to get a look. Now he's reaching into the second drawer of the bedside table.

This dildo is much bigger than the last one, and bright red. I watch in fascination as he lubes up the head and spreads it all over, so it shines in the light. Then Theo returns to his spot between my thighs, licking my clit a few times to get me wriggling and panting underneath him again.

"This might be uncomfortable at first," he says, prodding at my entrance with the slippery head. And he isn't lying. It spreads me wide, wider than I think I can possibly go. "It's all right," he whispers, lying down next to me so he can kiss my face while he works. "Take some deep breaths."

I try to do as I'm told, and one of his big arms curls around me as he starts to sink the dildo in. My hips wriggle, trying to escape this thick object that doesn't quite fit, so he stops and withdraws it.

"Try to relax," he says in a low rumble. "Pretend you're in a hot bath, with the jets on." I close my eyes and try to imagine it: all the tension flowing out of my body, all the anxiety leaving me as I trust in him. Slowly Theo dips in the narrow tip of the head, moving it in gentle circles, trying to widen me. When he presses the dildo into me a second time, all my skin stretches, and it feels like it might break me open.

"Theo," I whimper, my hips jerking of their own accord. "It hurts."

His face falls, and it's my worst worry come true: disappointing him. "Oh, sweetheart." He kisses my forehead, then nuzzles me with his wet nose. "I'm sorry." When he withdraws the dildo, my heart cracks down the middle. I wanted to be good. I wanted to take it, so that I could take *him*.

"Wait," I say. I can't fail at this. "Please, don't stop. I want to be ready for you."

A hand reaches under my chin, and Theo tilts it up so I'm

looking into his wide-set eyes, each so warm and full of affection for me—making it hurt even more that I couldn't go this next step with him.

"You'll be ready, I promise." He frowns when the tears finally work their way free and slip down my cheeks, and he wipes one away with his thumb. "Please don't worry. I'm not in a hurry, and I'm here with you every step of the way."

"What if it doesn't work, though?" I sniffle. What if I'm never able to be with him that way? I don't know what I'd do. He might not choose me in the end.

Theo sets the dildo aside and gathers me up in his arms. I can feel each of his steady breaths here, his soft fur rubbing my cheek like a downy blanket and soaking up my tears.

"It will." He rubs circles on my back as I cry harder. "We just have to take it nice and slow. Maybe it didn't fit this time, but your body will learn. Bodies are amazing like that—especially yours."

Though his words wash over me like warm water, I can't help dreading the idea that maybe this is for nothing and he's wasted all this effort on me.

"Hey." Theo brings his head down so his broad lips are right next to my ear. He combs one hand through my hair. "Even if that never happened between us, Celeste, I don't mind." He brings me in even closer. "You mean the world to me, and this doesn't change that. Not a bit."

My heart skips. I want to believe him. If anyone has shown me they can be trusted, it's Theo, and I know he wouldn't lie to me. I wind my arms around him as far as they can go and press my tear-streaked face into his chest fur.

"I care about you too," I murmur into him. "So much. I want to be right for you."

"You are right for me, sweetheart. Just the way you are."

When my crying has died down a little, Theo cleans up the

dildo in the sink and returns it to the drawer, bringing over a washcloth so he can dry my face. It's such a tender gesture that I almost want to cry all over again.

I don't know what I did to deserve this wonderful minotaur, and I think there's a good chance I'm falling in love with him.

Chapter Thirteen

It's finally Saturday, and even though I still feel anxious after last night, I'm thrilled to have two whole days with Theo before he has to go back to work. We've made all sorts of plans.

I get to have *plans* now. And for me, those plans include forgetting all about my attack and hopefully, ending up in Theo's bed so we can try out the big dildo again.

"I actually used to work Saturdays," Theo says, shaking his head with distaste as we hop into Donald Duck together.

"Oh?" The engine rolls over once before starting. "Why?"

"Didn't have anything else to do, so I... worked." He lets out a self-deprecating chuckle. "Kinda pathetic, huh?"

I reach across the console and squeeze his knee. "Not pathetic at all." It's one of the things I like about him: he's hard-working and dedicated.

Theo exhales like he's releasing built-up pressure. "But I'm psyched that I have you now. This is going to be a fun day, I think."

I know we're both thinking about the mummy, but neither of us says it. With Theo by me, I should have no reason to be afraid—and still, I can't help feeling trepidation as we pull up to the garden center to find it's overrun with monsters of all kinds, doing the same thing that we are.

Theo throws me a look. "You feeling up to this?"

"Yes." I'm intent on having a great day. "Let's go. Just..." I take one of his big fingers in my hand. "Don't lose me, okay?"

He nods solemnly. "I won't."

We get out of the truck, and Theo keeps one hand at the small of my back as we weave our way through the busy parking lot to the big greenhouse-like building. When we walk up, I'm hit in the face with the scent of flowers—and then actually by a mist of cold water, which makes me jump and splutter.

Inside, it all smells *green*. There are plants each place you look, crawling along the building supports, hanging from the ceiling in baskets, covering every surface. The walls are lined with racks of seeds, fertilizers, and tools. Theo lets go of me just long enough to get a cart. He leans over it, big nostrils flared, and lowers his head like a bull about to charge into a fight.

"Are you ready?" he asks, huffing.

Ready? "For what?"

"To go shopping!" He charges off with the cart, toward a big wall of trowels and hand rakes, and I go running after him, giggling. Theo starts picking things off the hangars. "We're going to need one of these, and definitely one of these." He drops in one of each. "What else, Celeste?"

"Plants!" I feel like a kid in a candy store, following along behind an even bigger kid with horns and a little swishy tail. "We came for plants, remember?"

"Of course. But you have to have the right tools for the job."

He gives a firm nod. "I can say from experience." Theo pulls down a kneepad and hands it to me. "Here. So you don't scratch up those cute little knees."

"Are you complimenting my *knees*?" I squish the pad and find myself giggling again.

"I sure am." Once again his hand falls to the small of my back. "I have no choice but to notice. They're adorable."

We make our way into the main garden area, where I see nothing but plants. Monsters are everywhere—some were-wolves tut over venus fly traps, a snakewoman scopes out the cilantro. I stay close to Theo's side as we brush past them with our cart.

"Pick out what you want," he says, gesturing to a big tray of seedlings. "We should probably get some basil. I love having fresh basil on pasta."

I like the idea of putting herbs in everything we cook, so I pick out a few different kinds before we move on to vegetables. After a while I stop noticing the other creatures around us because I'm so wrapped up in Theo and the giddy look on his face as we decide which kind of peppers to raise this year.

"I'm kind of a weenie about spicy stuff," he says. "So let's get some bell peppers, too."

"We'll fix that," I say. "It's something you have to work towards."

Theo gets a rakish look on his face, like he knows exactly what I'm talking about.

Finally we're checked out and headed back home. I roll down the truck window and let the breeze fling my hair around, enjoying the fresh summer air. Something was just so good and right about today that I hope that it never ends.

$\sim$

When we get home—and pulling up in front of the yellow house with the brick red shutters feels like coming home now— we unload all the goods, then get to work. Theo makes sure I'm drinking plenty of water as we labor under the sun, rigging the boxes with drip hoses and digging out neat holes for each of our new plants. As usual, Theo blasts metal, and I wonder what the plants will think of it.

When we're done, he looks over my idea for the hoop house, and promises to bring home wire we can use to create one.

"We just need some plastic sheeting, and I can probably get that at work, too," Theo says, rubbing his chin. "Shouldn't be too hard to build this."

"The tomatoes and the peppers will love it." I imagine how many big, fat tomatoes we could grow. How much pasta sauce could I make to serve with that basil?

"Let's go inside." Theo takes my hand in his and squeezes it. "It's hot out here, and I don't want you to get burned." He looks sheepish. "I kind of forgot human skin burns."

I laugh. "Oh, sheesh, so did I."

In the bathroom mirror I can tell I'm already starting to turn a little lobster-red.

"Hop on the couch," Theo tells me, and heads upstairs to grab something. He manages to dig out a bottle of aloe gel, and I take off my shirt so he can rub it into my fresh burns. The gentle motion turns into a deeper massage, with Theo's gigantic hands kneading all the muscles that I didn't realize had gotten sore from crouching down over the garden boxes.

"Guess I need to work on my posture when I'm out there," I say, letting out a little moan as Theo digs into a particularly knotty spot with his huge, strong thumb. Almost immediately I can feel him thicken up under his jeans right where my butt is perched on his thighs, and it sends a shiver rippling through me.

As sexy as it is knowing Theo's getting a boner for me, I'm also anxious. When we take off our clothes, we'll probably try the big red dildo again, and I don't want to fail a second time.

"Whoa." Theo stops moving his hands. "What happened, Celeste? You tensed up all over."

Oh. I try to exhale slowly and let my apprehension slide off of me. Theo told me we could take all the time in the world, that he still cared about me no matter what. I should be able to trust that, right?

Before I can say anything, Theo leans down and wraps his arms around me, tugging me back against his chest. He nudges the side of my face with his big nose. "Hey, sweetheart. We don't have to do anything you don't want to do."

How does he read my mind like that? "It's not about whether I want to," I say. "I want to, more than anything. But maybe that's why it didn't work. Maybe I'm trying too hard."

Theo nods in understanding. "I'm willing to wait as long as you need."

"I don't want to wait, though." I turn around in his arms so I'm straddling him, and that thick lump under his jeans twitches and swells. It's hot that I turn him on so much. "Can we... try again?"

A soft smile curls up his lips. "Of course." He shifts just a little so my ass is rubbing even more firmly against his cock, and his breath hitches. "I would love that. But can I make some dinner first after all the sweating we've done today?"

"I can't say no to a gorgeous minotaur who wants to cook for me." I rub his ears and kiss him on the nose.

"Good." He kisses me back, his hands roaming from my hips up to my chest, where he smooths them over my breasts.

My nipples peak under my bra from just that light touch. "I can't wait to get your clothes off later."

We cook pasta with store-bought tomatoes, and I can't wait until we make it with our own instead. I add some fresh basil on top while Theo pours out wine.

"Fancy!" I say. It's a brisk white with a fruity finish, and it pairs perfectly with our food. By the end of the meal I'm feeling much more relaxed, and quite a bit frisky. I want to get my minotaur upstairs in front of those mirrors again, preferably without his jeans on.

I get out of my chair, and Theo quirks an eyebrow when I offer him my hand.

"Will you take me to the bedroom, my valiant steed?" I ask, giggling. I can't hold it in.

He grins a wide grin. "Thought some wine might help your nerves." He gets up too, towering over me while still holding onto my hand. "I'd love to."

Suddenly, he reaches under my knees and picks me up, just like he did on our second date.

I wiggle in his arms. "I can walk, you know!"

"Sure, but you did just call me your steed." Theo winks. "I can't be falling down on the job."

My laugh comes out a snort as he carries me up the stairs, and at that, he guffaws.

"You're so cute, Celeste." He takes a swift left turn at his bedroom door. "I love making you laugh."

And I love his bedroom, I decide then. The sheets are soft as silk, and in the morning, the light that comes in the window makes me feel cozy and happy. Not to mention the mirrors where I can see everything, including Theo's wide, muscled back and cute, twitching tail.

He kisses me on the forehead before settling me onto the bed. I'm so eager to see him again that I reach under his shirt and pull it up right away, and he chuckles at me. I can't help it —I adore his body and how his big chest billows out into his powerful belly, all of it covered in velvety white fur. While Theo takes off his shirt, I unbutton my own and toss it to the side. With wine flowing through my bloodstream I feel loose and free, and all I want is to be close to my minotaur, as close as I possibly can be. Once my shirt's gone, I go for my leggings, peeling them off in a very unsexy, ungainly kind of way, but I know Theo won't judge me for it. No, he's already kicking off his jeans with his hooves, sending them into a corner of the room where hopefully he won't need them again until tomorrow.

Then his underwear comes down, and that incredible cock of his is revealed to me again. With courage fueled by the wine, I reach out for it and wrap both hands around it, and Theo's big, dark eyes go wide.

"Do you like it?" he asks with a sultry little smile.

"I love it." Stroking him, I lead him back toward the bed, and he falls down onto it. Seeing him sprawled out before me, his belly moving in time with his heavy breaths, his big horns curling up on either side of his head, I'm so turned on that I wish I could take him inside me right now.

But the steps. I have to do the steps.

I explore his cock more, sitting over him so I can better get my hands around it. Theo grunts when I venture lower, investigating his big, furry balls underneath. They tighten up when I touch them, and his cock spasms in my hand.

"Sweetheart," he says, gazing up at me with those gentle eyes, "I want to touch you." He opens one arm to invite me into it, so I cuddle up next to him, not taking my hands off that incredibly hot, solid length. His hands find their way to my breasts, then my nipples, gently rolling them until they're hard as stones. Then he reaches down between my legs, and my thighs part for him.

"Ahh." He huffs into my hair with pleasure as his hand ducks between them. "You're already so wet. Is that all for me?"

"It's all for you." Theo rewards me with a groan, and I'm happy to have pleased him. His hand glides up and down, testing out every inch of me, circling my clit and then flicking it back and forth, dipping inside me and stroking there, too. His finger doesn't feel nearly as big as it used to, and I hope that means tonight will go better.

Even though I'm eager to start, I stay by Theo's side, never taking my hands off of him. A bead of white pre-come has spilled through the slit at the tip of his cock, showing me just how excited he is for me, but he doesn't stop teasing. He kisses my head, murmuring, "You're so beautiful, Celeste. I love the way you touch me." Soon he slips two fingers inside me, probing and urging me open.

"Am I ready yet?" I ask, gasping when they curl and find that sensitive spot along my inner wall.

"Almost." Then Theo's between my legs, hitching my thighs up over his biceps, and I know he's going to use that incredible textured tongue on me again. His cool nose rubs over my pussy, and he lets out a gratified exhale. "You smell wonderful, Celeste." I let out a whimper in response.

Then the tongue comes out. He licks my clit, taunting it, swirling it around and around until I'm wriggling and moaning and he's holding on tight to my legs to keep me in place. Theo doesn't relent, tormenting every part of me with that amazing wide tongue. He curls it and shoves it inside me, and I'm shocked at how easily it fits.

When I'm close to the edge, gripping his horns with both hands while I try to stay rooted to earth, Theo slows down and drops my legs back down to the bed. I whimper in protest.

He kisses up my belly to my breasts. "We don't want you too tight."

Reaching into the bedside table, he takes out the blue dildo, the one I know I can take.

"I don't think I'll need lube with how wet you are," Theo says with a grin.

I shake my head. I want it inside me, now.

Chapter Fourteen

In the reflection in the mirror, I watch Theo's incredible ass flex as he brings the dildo down between my legs, his tail flicking quickly back and forth with anticipation. The head easily fits inside me, and Theo lets out a gratified sigh. "You're so soft for me now," he says, working it in a little at a time before taking it back out again, just teasing me. It slides in and out easily, whisked along by how wet Theo has gotten me, leaving nothing but pleasure in its wake.

It isn't long before the dildo is all the way in, and Theo starts to thrust with abandon. His hand drops down to his own cock, and his eyes find mine as he strokes himself in the same rhythm. I'm enraptured by his big, dark eyes, the shocks of white in his eyebrows, the way his big nostrils flare with every one of his heavy breaths. The dildo feels wonderful, but watching Theo's cock swell in his hands, I think I want more.

Once I'm moaning and bucking my hips in time with the dildo, he slows down and withdraws it. My own juices drip in rivulets down the silicone as he sets it on the dresser. Theo releases his cock, but it still stands at attention while he reaches into the drawer and withdraws the red toy again. He covers it in lube, and once it's slick and shining, he draws my legs apart so I'm splayed out in front of him. He gently turns me on the bed so my pussy is aimed straight at the mirrors, and leans down to bring his mouth to my ear.

"Watch," he whispers, and shivers spread across my skin.

So I do. I watch as he brings the huge round head to my slit, where he ever-so-slowly nudges it inside. Again my body tries to stretch, and sensing resistance, he withdraws the dildo just a little, then slides only the head back in, over and over. I can feel myself slowly parting for it, but it's stretching me as far as I can go. I wriggle a little under his hands and Theo pauses.

"Does it hurt?" he asks, bringing his fingers to my clit and teasing me there while the dildo waits patiently.

I shake my head furiously. "No. Not yet."

"Good." Once again he tests me, pushing the head further in, and I can see it spreading my swollen lower lips wide as it works its way inside. He strokes just that head in and out, loosening me up even more, and soon the discomfort morphs into an incredible, eye-popping pleasure.

"There we are," he croons, and kisses my face again as he presses it further in. I can't believe there's more, but looking in the mirror, I can tell I've only taken part of the head, and the rest of that long, slick shaft still remains. I'm trembling in anticipation, wondering how it will all feel.

But Theo is in no rush. He lies down next to me, his hooves hanging off the bed as he continues lavishing attention on my clit and pumping just the tip in and out of me. Every stroke unleashes another torrent of pleasure, twisting me up and up, higher and higher. I almost don't notice when he pushes it further inside because my body eagerly brings it in, giving underneath the thick shaft. I watch in the mirror as it slowly disappears inside me, and I'm astonished that I can take it all.

Before I know it, I've swallowed the entire thing. When the head starts to rub against my most sensitive spot, my pussy is spread so wide and full that it can barely clench.

I moan and bury my face in Theo's shoulder, squeezing his furry bicep tight as he starts to gently pump the dildo inside me. As I get wetter and wetter, his strokes speed up, and soon my whole body is responding to each thrust as the toy fucks me. I'm moaning something incoherent, like I'm possessed. Theo brings his other hand back to my clit, and instantaneously I'm climaxing, each heavy stroke of the dildo drawing me higher and higher. I scream as all of my muscles squeeze tight, and Theo just maintains his pace until there are tears bursting from my eyes.

Finally, it's over, and my chest is heaving as he gently withdraws the toy. It's soaked when Theo sets it on the bedside table next to the first, smaller one. And it doesn't compare to the size of the huge cock between his haunches that's still hard and thick.

When I've finally regained my breath, Theo brings me into his arms and fervently kisses the top of my head.

"You did so well, sweetheart," he says, running a hand through my hair. "So well."

"Am I ready yet?" I ask.

"Yes." Theo traces my hip, and I wonder if he's imagining what we'll do together just as vividly as I am. "Tomorrow, we'll give it a try."

Relief and happiness and desire all course through me at once. "Good."

When I can move again, I take his cock in my hands, sucking it as far as I can fit it into my mouth, funneling all my adoration and affection into my tongue and lips. The tenor of Theo's grunts climbs until he's lowing deep and loud, his hips thrusting into my hands while I drag my tongue all over his wide, soft head.

"Fuck, sweetheart," he groans. "That's so damn good." He swells up under my hands, and lets out a final bellow as he releases into my mouth. I swallow until I can't anymore, but he's still spilling out on my face. When we're done, he gapes at how much come he's covered me in.

"Wow," he says, wiping at my lips with a tissue and then kissing me. "You really pull it all out of me."

Once I'm cleaned off, we curl up together, and in the darkness I feel Theo lipping my hair.

"That toy looked so hot inside you," he murmurs, and I raise a hand to run it up and down his big muzzle. "I can't wait until it's me."

I sigh into his chest. "Me, too."

I'm a little sore now, but it will feel better in the morning. Then I get to finally have him.

It's Sunday, our last day together before Theo has to go back to work tomorrow. When I open my eyes, someone is kissing my ear, my cheek, my jaw, and I think I would very much enjoy waking up like this every day.

After making out like horny teenagers, we finally get up and dress. I realize I've barely used the room that Theo so thoughtfully set up and decorated for me, but I'm all right with that. I like his bed much better.

In the warm light coming through the kitchen window, he makes us a pancake breakfast with eggs and sausage-seasoned mushrooms. I barely notice that I don't eat much meat anymore because he's so good at cooking without it. Then we climb into Donald Duck and head to the nursing home.

I'm looking forward to seeing Daphne again. Things have changed quickly between Theo and I since the last time we visited, and I want to get to know her even more, this person who's so important to him.

We stop on the way to get some new flowers, and I try to pick out something bright that I think she'll like. Maybe a part of me is excited to see her again because she reminds me of Julianne, and I'll never feel like I got enough time with her.

Daphne is, once again, delighted to see her grandson. Theo shuffles over to hug her, and when she sees me, her face lights up.

"You'll have to forgive me," she says, ushering me over for a hug, too. "But I don't remember your name."

"Celeste."

She nods and repeats it. "Celeste. Right." Theo dumps out the vase, removes the old flowers and puts in the new ones, then refreshes the water. "How is the trial marriage going, Celeste?"

I can't help glancing over at Theo, thinking about what we did last night. "It's going really well," I tell her, sitting next to the bed. "We built a garden, and we just planted it yesterday."

Daphne gets a wide smile on her face that reminds me of Theo's. "That's a rather permanent thing, isn't it?" she says with a waspish look at her grandson.

He scratches the back of his head, a gesture I've come to adore. "I guess it is. I've always liked the idea, but Celeste is really passionate about it. She loves plants."

Daphne nods knowingly. "I see you both have a nurturing personality. That's good. You'll always take care of each other."

I feel like Theo does most of the caretaking—but maybe I do give him something back. The satisfaction he gets from doing it, from taking me new places and cooking me food and guiding my body, seems like enough for him.

When Theo's done with the flowers, Daphne gestures for him to sit down, too.

"So how are you enjoying the big wide world, dear?" she asks me. With a wink at Theo she says, "I hope he's taking you lots of fun and interesting places."

I'm not sure how to answer at first. I love living with Theo, and I enjoyed going to the nursery. But I still can't forget the gaping holes in the mummy's face.

"It's... it's so *much*." I hadn't really put it into words before, but that's the only way I can. "There are monsters everywhere. I'm still not really used to it."

Daphne nods. "Of course not. It will take time. But you have Theo with you, don't you?" He slides an arm around my shoulders and gives me a gentle squeeze.

I know I do. But I worry about Maddie, somewhere out there going to the grocery store alone. About the mummy's rotting face.

"I was actually thinking..." Theo begins, trailing a hand down my arm. "What if we went on a little trip? You've seen plenty of the city now, and I thought maybe you'd want to, um, explore some more."

I *love* this idea. Immediately I want to get in the truck or hop on a plane and go somewhere with Theo. See a new place, anywhere outside the city that's different and new.

Then slimy dread crawls up from my belly. What if Theo had to leave me for a few minutes to go to the bathroom? What if we got separated at the busy airport? There are so many possible scenarios where I end up on my own in a strange place, where some creature can find me and devour me.

I imagine how Theo would feel finding my body, and I want to cry.

"Um," is all I manage to answer as Theo and Daphne both look at me expectantly. "Y-yeah. Going on a trip would be fun."

Theo's face falls at my lack of enthusiasm, and instantly, I feel terrible.

"Maybe it's too soon," Daphne says, reaching out to pat my arm. "You're still figuring it out. Adapting. It takes a while."

I nod quickly. "Yes, that's it. I just need time, and then I'd love to travel somewhere with you, Theo." That's partially true. I don't know if any amount of time will make a difference.

Theo nods slowly, but I can tell by his raised eyebrow that we'll be talking more about this later.

The rest of our visit with Daphne is lovely, and she insists on a full run-down of all the plants we'll be growing this year. She forgets my name on the way out, then hugs me again.

"Give him a chance to be there for you," she says quietly while Theo heads to the door. She pats me on the back. "All right, you two. I'll see you next week."

Chapter Fifteen

When we hop in the truck, we hold hands, and as always, mine disappears into his huge palm.

"I'm sorry," Theo says after a time, turning down the music so we can hear ourselves talk over it. "I put you on the spot about the trip."

I cringe knowing that I hurt him. "No, I'm sorry. I should have been more excited when you suggested it."

"Hey." He squeezes my thigh and looks at me out of the side of his eye. "You don't have to put on an act for me. That's not like you. I want to know how you really feel so I can help you through whatever's bothering you."

What did I do to deserve him?

"I'm afraid." There. I've put the words out there. "What if something happens? I could be waiting outside a bathroom for you and a werewolf decides to tear out my vocal cords."

Theo shudders. "That's vivid. I can see why you'd be scared. But I won't let that happen."

"There are some things outside of your control." Maybe I'm afraid because the simple truth is that there are times and places where Theo can't truly protect me the way he does everywhere else—in the bedroom, in our life. There are places in the world where the bubble of safety around him ends.

"This is true," he says. "But you also don't know what wonderful things you might miss if you don't take a risk." Suddenly, he pulls over to the side of the road, and turns to me. He leans over and kisses me with surprising roughness, his arms wrapping around me tight as he fully takes over my mouth. By the way he kisses me, I know that he would do anything for me. I can feel it in my marrow.

He pulls away, breathing raggedly. "It's selfish of me," he says. "I want to take you so many places. I love seeing you get excited when we go to a new restaurant. I love how much fun we had at the garden center. There's so much joy I want to show you and experience with you."

This time it's my turn to kiss Theo, because otherwise I might cry, and I'd rather kiss than cry. I pour everything I feel about him into it, how his deep kindness and sincerity makes me perfectly at ease with him.

I've enjoyed everything I've experienced since I left New Eden. If this is just what the yellow house with the red shutters has to offer, I try to imagine what greater joys there might be out in the world. Maybe it would be worth the risk if I get to do it with Theo. I loved the way he ran through the nursery like a little boy.

"I don't think that's selfish," I say. "I want to experience it all with you, too." And it's true. The pleasures of the world would all be so much better if we were doing it together.

After one more hungry kiss, Theo puts the truck in drive. Maybe he's right. Moving in with him was a risk. Putting my heart in his hands was a risk. Perhaps every day is a risk, to some degree or another, and if I want to enjoy Theo fully I'll have to be willing to take them.

Our next stop is an outdoor movie at a big amphitheater, and Theo pulls me into his lap to give me a nice, soft seat. There are some witches next to us with their familiars, one of them a very large puma. On the other side sit a pair of orcs, clearly out on a date, too. They eye me once, but Theo makes it clear that I'm his, and they don't look over again.

It's an action movie, so I can let my mind go while I enjoy the visuals. I snuggle into Theo's warm chest, wishing he wasn't wearing a shirt so I could feel all of his soft fur. I think about what will come later, and he must be thinking about it, too, because it's not long before I feel something growing under my thighs.

"I can smell it, you know," he whispers, tucking his head over my shoulder. "When you get turned on." I rub my cheeks as my face instantly turns red.

"I... uh..." That's humiliating. I wonder if the orcs can smell it, too.

Theo chuckles and rubs his snout against my face. "I'm excited for later."

When the movie's finally over, I'm sweating from the heat and my need to get him home with me. All I can think about is how that big, red dildo felt when he finally got it inside, and I know Theo will feel even better—soft and smooth and pliable in all the right ways.

Then we're parking in the driveway, I think that it really does feel like home now.

Once we're inside, Theo takes my arm and spins me around

until I'm up against the door, his elbows bracketing my face. He drops his mouth close to mine, and nibbles at my lower lip.

"I can barely wait," he murmurs, stroking the side of my face. "I haven't thought about anything but being inside you all day."

Instantly my blood turns to lava. I want Theo more than I've ever wanted anything. He's just what I'd hoped for, and so much more than that.

"Theo." I stroke his hair, then his long ear. It flicks under my hand as he listens closely. "I want you to know how much I care about you. How much I appreciate everything you've done to make me feel welcome here. How you've brought me into your life. I really..." My voice falters. "I really like it here."

Theo lets out a relieved breath and leans his forehead against the wall above my head.

"I'm glad it's not only me. You just fit here. When you came in the front door that first time, I felt like it was all how it's supposed to be."

My fingers glide over the side of his muzzle, under his jaw, down his throat. I like the idea that I could keep enjoying Theo forever. That would be a good life.

"I know what you mean," I say. I felt it, too, when we first drove up to the house—an inkling that I probably wasn't going to be leaving again.

I wind my way further down his belly, to the thicker fur poking out of his jeans. While we're here having this much-needed conversation, I don't want him to forget what else he wants tonight.

"I don't want to influence your decision—" Theo sticks on his words for a moment as I graze over his crotch and down to his thigh, "—about whether or not to stay. But I hope that you stay."

My heart flies up into my throat, like it's grown wings. Oh, I want nothing else more than to be here, with him.

"I would love to stay," I say, my voice choking up with emotion. "Right here."

All at once I'm wrapped up in Theo. He buries his head in my hair and squeezes me tight, so tight I almost can't breathe. Then he leans down and slides one of his big hands under my legs, sweeping me up off my feet and into his arms. He takes the stairs two at a time, and again the bedroom door bumps into the wall when he opens it.

I giggle. "We have to get you one of those bumper thingies."

"Me?" He falls back onto the bed with me still planted in his lap. "Us. We'll have to get *us* one of those bumper thingies. Put it on the shopping list." Already he's kissing down my throat, lavishing me in attention with his lips and tongue. He's quick to pull my dress up over my head, and he groans when he sees me.

"Celeste," he whispers, drinking me in with his eyes. "From the stars." He plucks off my bra, and his mouth descends on my nipples. Teasing and taunting them, he shows me just how else he'll worship my body. His hand slips into my panties—I wore the nicest ones I had, with some lace trim around the edge— and dives right into sampling me, sliding around to see how wet I am for him.

Good. He's eager, too.

"We'll have to go slow," Theo says, almost as much for himself as for me. His finger dips in, testing me, and then another fits easily. But I don't want to go slow. I want to finally have him inside me, to join our bodies together, to be fully surrounded by him. Yet he keeps teasing me with just two fingers, slicking in and out of me, stopping from time to time to graze over my clit. I'm starting to fly already but I want more, and more. I'm so empty, and I know there's only one cure.

While Theo's busy in my underwear I pull up his shirt, savoring the softness of his white belly hair. "Will you take off your clothes?" I ask him.

"Whatever you want, sweetheart." He kicks off his pants and pulls his shirt up over his horns. Finally he's bared completely for me, from his powerful shoulders to his heavy pecs, to the big, firm belly. Even his furry thighs are thick and powerful, and my whole body tightens just thinking about them flexing as he thrusts his cock inside of me.

Once my underwear are gone, it's just us again with nothing else keeping our bodies apart. We wrap around each other, an inextricable tangle of arms and legs, my thighs cradling his hips so that big cock is trapped against my wet, hot center. Theo groans and rubs against me, spreading my wetness all over himself.

"Slow," he repeats, closing his eyes for a moment as if meditating. I think this is the first time I've ever seen Theo get close to losing control. He's so calm, so shy, so self-assured that the idea never even occurred to me. After a deep breath, he retreats down my body, tasting every part of me, and my legs open for him. Then he's licking me, his wet nose brushing my clit as he ducks down and presses his huge tongue inside me, lathering me up for him.

Once I'm squirming and moaning, he reaches for the bedside table and pulls out the first blue dildo. He doesn't even need to lube it up to slide it inside me because I'm already dripping all over the bed from his labors. I feel it, but it's not nearly as intense as before, and still I want more—but I try to remember what he said about taking it slow. In the mirror I watch Theo sitting back on his haunches, his cock already thick and starting to leak. He takes it in one hand while he fucks me with the dildo, faster and faster, until I'm crying out and pushing back against it to take it as deep as I can.

Theo has a knowing smile on his face as he gradually slows down. He removes the blue dildo, setting it on the bedside table. Then he brings out the red one.

After covering it in lube, he circles my entrance with it at first, getting a sense of how tight I still am. The head eases inside, and I'm surprised at how quickly I part and widen for it. After a few shallow thrusts it settles deep inside me, and I gasp as my body accommodates. Theo's eyes are fixated on mine, and white pre-come is now dripping in a steady stream from his cock. It's bigger than I've ever seen it, swelled up with all of the blood his body has funneled to it. Once the dildo starts to move, all I can think about is that cock instead, and I moan and writhe under its steady strokes.

Theo sees the look on my face and smiles that warm, pleased smile I'm coming to love so much. He pumps the dildo inside me faster and faster, pausing from time to time to plunge it deep and run it back and forth over my innermost parts. I feel white hot, ready to burst into flames, but still I want more. Theo works me until I feel like I might simply pop—but before I can hit the edge, he pulls it out gently and sets it on the bedside table.

"How did I do?" I ask, panting from my near-orgasm.

"Wonderfully, sweetheart." He kisses my forehead, my nose, my mouth. "You're ready now."

Chapter Sixteen

Theo drags his hands down my body as he finds his place between my legs, kneeling with his huge cock sticking straight out toward me. I don't know how he'll fit, but somehow, he will. We've both been patient, and I've already worked so hard to be prepared for him.

He brings out lube again, and he spreads it all over his cockhead. Then he guides it down, and in the mirror I can see what he sees. The head slides between my folds, rubbing over my clit and spreading his pre-come and the lube all over me. Desperately wanting more of him, I lift my hips, and he slides down so he's pressed against my slit.

"It will be uncomfortable at first," Theo warns me. "But I'll go very slow." As much as I don't want that, as much as I want him to shove himself inside me and finally fit where he belongs, I know after all we've done that he's right.

Finally, with a hungry kiss on my lips, he obliges. That huge, dark head starts to nudge its way inside, and I feel it stretching me, widening me—but I'm so wet that it slides through. I gasp and clutch the pillow when it meets my first layer of resistance, and Theo takes a halting breath. He's stretching me as far as I can possibly go, until there's no more give left.

"Sweetheart, you feel so good." He leans down and nuzzles my face, leaving kisses all down my cheek. "Try to relax. Look at me, and let it all go."

So I do what I'm told and raise my eyes to his. They're soft and dark with bottomless affection as he covers my body with his hands, caressing my breasts, squeezing my hips, letting me know how he cares for me. That's when my channel finally softens, and with the utmost gentleness, he slides further inside.

"Oh!" I grip his shoulders, digging my fingers into his fur. I feel so full already that I don't know how he could possibly fit more, but as Theo strokes my hair, murmuring sweet things in my ear, he does. When I let out a sharp gasp he pauses, then withdraws just a little, letting my body adjust. He repeats this motion over and over, and I'm so wet that he has no trouble moving in and out, just an inch or two deep. That wide head stimulates every nerve ending, and each time he wades back in, I moan and clench Theo even tighter.

"I need you, Theo," I manage out, bucking my hips in hope of taking more of him in. "I need you so badly."

When he smiles at me it's like a warm, sunny day. "I've needed you my whole life." He gets as close to me as he can, holding himself up on just his elbows, brushing his nose over my face. "You ready to let me in?"

I try to relax, urging myself to give, to let him through. Finally, my body listens. "Yes," I moan. "Please, come in."

Then Theo plunges the rest of the way inside me. I can't help the cry I let out as at last, he fills me up, settling in a deep place that feels like it was reserved just for him. Every part of me is stretching, shifting to make room, and Theo lets out a deep, relieved sigh.

"You're so perfect," he says, kissing my forehead and cradling my face in his hands. "Kind and wonderful and lovely. Everything I could've wanted."

Tears build behind my eyes because I know now that this is where I'm meant to be. Everything inside me is calling Theo's name as he slowly pulls himself out, so we're just barely connected. Once more he slides in, and this time it's smooth as butter as he returns to that same wonderful spot, right where he belongs.

My minotaur continues his slow, methodical pace, filling me up completely and then withdrawing until I'm begging for him to return. He makes love to me—that's what this is, I can feel it—the same way he does everything: paying close attention, acting intentionally and thoughtfully. Each stroke delivers a burst of pleasure that starts in my abdomen, lancing out across my body. His huge cockhead brushes past that sensitive place deep down and I writhe and moan underneath him, my thighs gripping tight around his hips.

Oh, my Theo, who somehow knows just what I need.

"Is that good?" he asks, a look of mischief in his eye. All I can do is nod because the words are trapped in some other part of my brain. "Good," he says, running his big nose over my hair and kissing it. He turns to look at us in the mirror and whispers, "Look."

I drink in the sight of him on top of me, his cock emerging only to vanish inside me again. I can't even take all of his length, and the sight of our bodies moving together, his powerful ass tensing with each thrust, threatens to send me plummeting off a cliff.

Again and again Theo slides in, filling me up, completing me, and soon I'm crying out his name, gripping tightly around his neck, wishing I could simply merge my body with his and become one. As my pleasure grows, Theo lets out a moan of his own, and he rests his forehead against mine.

"I can't believe I found you," he murmurs, stroking inside me with the slow, sure rocking of his big furry haunches. "You mean everything to me."

"Oh, Theo." My head falls back to the pillow, lost as I am in the feeling of him, in the warmth of his words. "I want you. Every moment of every day, I want you with me."

He groans and sinks in deep, taking me, owning me, making me his. Before long, I'm so slick that his huge cock makes a slurping noise with every thrust, his heavy sac brushing against my ass as he buries himself completely in my body. It feels like static electricity is slowly building inside me, tingling every inch of my skin, making me ache for release. Theo sits back on his haunches as he continues his exploration of me, and brings his hand down to where my swollen lips are spread wide around him. First he pauses to coat his fingers in our juices, then I feel his hand brush over my clit.

My hips snap hard, and all of my muscles clench tight as this new sensation takes me over. Theo grits his teeth like he's struggling to hold something back, and he slows his hips as his hand speeds up. That wonderful ache is expanding, swallowing me, wrapping me up in fine, soft linen. I clutch the pillow in my hands as he starts to move again, and I'm so tight that each thrust is like a firework going off behind my eyes.

"I'm so close," I whimper, feeling tears building behind my eyes. I might just explode. "Please, Theo. Please."

He growls, a guttural sound I haven't heard him make before, and obliges. Soon he's pounding me, plundering my slick pussy with all the power stored in those thick thighs and that perfect ass. This is the beastly side, the animal side taking over all his conscious thought. I'm writhing, crying out as his hand speeds up and his cock fills me to bursting... and then I'm there.

I scream as the lightning finally strikes, a sharp bolt from the place where our bodies connect all the way up into my throat. I'm clenching and squeezing and Theo lets out a helpless low as he shoves through all of it, and then, he can't hold back any longer. The tears stream from my eyes as he slams himself in, swelling up thick, filling me up as much as he can, and lets go.

His explosion is so powerful I feel it strike me deep inside, his hot come filling any small gap that might remain. My back arches as the tsunami continues, rippling through me. Theo falls forward, burying his face in my neck.

Finally, the sheer power of my climax eases and I can almost breathe normally again. Theo grunts, keeping one arm under him so he doesn't crush me.

"Oh, sweetheart," he says, voice cracking. "You're so wonderful. And so perfect for me."

I hold his head in both hands, smoothing down his ears, his cheek, his long nose. A sense of satisfaction seeps in as I realize that this marvelous creature is mine, all mine, and this is just the beginning.

We lie like that for what feels like eons, his softening length still inside me, his come spilling down my ass and onto the comforter.

"Theo?" I ask, after the hurricane finally ebbs.

"Yes?" He props his head up on his elbow so he can look in my eyes, and there's a honey-sweetness pooled in those dark irises.

"I think I might be in love with you."

His smile is so soft, so genuine that I think I'm going to cry. Again.

"I'm definitely in love with you," he says, brushing some hair back from my face. "I probably have been for a while."

It's been fast, sure—but when you know, you know.

He shifts so we're lying side-by-side, and slowly his huge cock slides out of me. All that hard work paid off, and I want nothing else but to be filled with him forever.

We make love many more times that night, even though Theo has to get up early for work in the morning.

"I don't think I'll be able to walk tomorrow," I joke.

"That's okay." He tucks me neatly into the crook of his neck. "Just lay in bed and watch TV, so you'll be ready again when I get home."

I laugh. "So I'm your sex toy now?"

Theo looks offended. "I'm actually hoping you'll be my wife, instead."

I fall silent at this. This is bigger than asking me to stay. This is forever.

He tenses up when I don't say anything. "Celeste?" he asks nervously.

"You want to marry me?" I reach up to wipe my face as tears have already started streaming down. How come I always cry around Theo? Knowing he feels the same way about me fills my heart to the brim, and I'm spilling over the top. "Really?"

He pulls me closer. "Oh, sweetheart. Of course I do. I want you to plant your garden. Cook meals with me. Sleep next to me every night. I want to take care of you forever."

He says every word I've been wishing to hear, and so many more I didn't know I wanted until now. I bury my face in his furry chest as I cry, and he doesn't have to ask if they're sad or happy tears. He just strokes my hair while I let it all out.

Finally I've recovered enough to answer him. "Yes," I whisper as I rub my face, which is now red and itchy. "I want all that, too. Please."

I don't need to see his face to know he's smiling that shy, pleased smile of his. His hot breath ruffles my hair. "Thank you for making me the happiest minotaur in the whole world."

We're both so sticky with sweat and Theo's come that we have to get into the shower. He takes me against the tile wall, just like I'd imagined. Under the shower head, pressed up against my minotaur's big body, I'm giddy just imagining what the future has in store for us.

Chapter Seventeen

When I walk into the cafeteria at New Eden a few days later, Rob looks up in surprise.

"You're back?" he asks. His face falls. "Didn't work out?"

"The opposite." I sit down across from him, grinning like an idiot. "I'm moving out. Theo asked me to marry him."

Victorious, Rob slaps the table. "Ha! How about that." He looks me up and down. "You seem pretty happy."

"I am." I scratch the back of my head, just like Theo does. "Happier than I could ever imagine."

It's strange packing up the rest of my things, knowing I'm saying goodbye to the preserve for good. There are other people who live here wishing for their happily ever after, and I hope they're all able to find something as wonderful and right as what I found with Theo.

Rob helps me get the rest of my stuff out of my house, and I give him a big hug goodbye.

"Are things going well with Rassa?" I ask.

He smiles. "Yeah. Maybe I'll do the trial marriage like you soon, too."

Then it's time to fill out paperwork. Theo joins me in the office, barely fitting into the chair they've given him as we sign our names on the paperwork.

"Remember that trip I mentioned?" Theo asks as we load the rest of my bags into the back of the truck.

"Yes." I wonder where he wanted to take us.

"I had been thinking, um, maybe that could be our honeymoon?"

Traveling for our honeymoon? I feel like I'm floating the moment he says it. Maybe it's a risk, but I know that if I'm with Theo, I'll be all right.

"Where do you want to go?" I ask.

"What do you think of Canada? I'll have my neighbor watch the dogs and the garden while we're gone. The yeti, remember? He's the one who told me the spot we should check out."

Canada feels close enough that it's safe, and far enough that it's exotic.

"All right." I wrap my arm around his bicep and lean into him as he starts up Donald Duck. "I'd love that."

The first thing we do is move all of my things into our bedroom, and turn the second room into an office and studio, with space by the window to sprout seedlings. When we get back from our honeymoon, I'll be starting part-time work as a remote assistant. Theo brought home a painting tarp for my easel, so I never have to worry about my cup of water spilling over.

Maddie and Egorr meet me at the bridal shop, with the goal of picking out a dress that's sure to blow Theo away. It'll be a small wedding in the backyard, because we'd both rather save our money for traveling in the winter and making our garden even bigger and better, and neither of us has much in the way of family.

"We might even remodel the kitchen," I tell Maddie as I try on a third dress. She laces up the back for me and the attendant clips it tight to show off my curves. "It's a little past its prime, and we'll need more space for the amount of canning we want to do in the fall."

My friend grins at me, and leads me out of the dressing room to the platform in front of the mirrors. They make me think of Theo's bedroom—*our* bedroom—and all the things we can watch ourselves do there.

"I'm so happy you found your place," Maddie says, turning me around in front of the mirrors. The dress swings low, dipping between my breasts before coming back together in a keyhole. "I think you and Theo will be really happy."

Thinking about everything we have planned for our lives together, I agree.

"I even took the dogs on a walk alone," I tell her. She beams at me.

"That's a big step. And everything went okay?"

"Just fine." The kind, neighborly yeti even waved at me, and we held a nice conversation while the dogs tried to drag me to the park. I love going places with Theo, but I don't always need him. He's happier knowing I can go out on my own, even if it's just for a few minutes at a time.

When I've tried on my fourth dress, I gape at myself in the mirror. "This is the one," I say, spinning in a circle. The dress doesn't have a train, because I know the dogs will run all over it. It has some lace but no rhinestones, and feels like just the right amount of everything for me.

"Who's going to be there?" Maddie asks as the attendant takes my measurements.

"His grand-dam, Daphne, an uncle who's coming from

Maine, some cousins he hasn't seen in a decade... and a guy from work." Doug is the only wild card, but Theo assures me he's had his need for devouring brains under control for five years. "It'll be good practice for me, I think."

Egorr has been standing outside to keep an eye on things, but he leans in the door when he sees me in the dress and gives me a thumbs up to encourage my decision.

"Theo's going to faint," he says.

Maddie nods rapidly. "You'll absolutely blow his socks off with this. Do minotaurs wear socks? He probably doesn't need socks."

On the big day, one of the women from New Eden comes to do my makeup. Theo and I made a loose promise not to see each other once we were dressed, and I'm hopping from one foot to the other just thinking about what he'll look like in a tux.

"Stay still," Penelope says. "I'm trying to get this eyeliner just right."

I wait inside the house until Bug and Ramona come to get me, the rings tied around their necks. When I step out onto the back porch, I hear Theo's gasp, and I know I picked the right dress.

He looks even better than I expected. He wears a classic black bowtie, and his suit is perfectly tailored to his huge shoulders. I don't even hide how hungry I am as I look him over from horns to hooves.

My minotaur.

He's holding a hand out to me when I walk up beside him in front of our officiant, who was sent by New Eden. A farewell present.

"Celeste," Theo says, taking both my hands. "You really are

a gift from the stars. More than I ever could've dreamed of. I'm so happy I get to share my life with you."

I came up with vows and memorized them, but now they've completely fled my mind as my eyes well up with tears. Theo brushes them away, smiling fondly down at me, and all I can think to say is, "I love you, Theo, more than any star in the sky."

Unfortunately, Theo's uncle has to chase after the dogs when they spot a squirrel and take off running. But eventually we do get to exchange our rings, and when it's time to kiss, Theo lifts me up off the ground like the first time he kissed me outside the preserve, and as I wrap my hands around his neck and kiss him back with all the love in my heart, I think that I'm quite possibly the luckiest human who ever lived.

I meet Doug at the reception, and he's quite kind to me. I don't shy away from him despite the fact his skin of his jaw is missing and you can see his tongue flap as he talks. Then I spend some time with Daphne.

"You're beautiful, darling," she says, kissing my cheek. "Welcome to the family. I'm so glad you have each other."

It's wonderful to be back with Rob and Maddie again. It's almost like I never left New Eden at all. We promise to get together many times more, hopefully out in the real world.

But I'm dying to be alone with Theo, and then get on our way to our honeymoon. Eventually everyone files out, but I'm so tired already I could almost keel over.

As if sensing how exhausted I am, Theo hefts me up into his arms.

"Oh?" I ask, rubbing my cheek on his big chest.

"Mm hmm," he answers, kissing the top of my head as he

carries me up the stairs. "Isn't it traditional to carry the bride over the threshold?"

He steps gingerly into our bedroom, then sets me down on the bed. He takes off his jacket, then unbuttons his dress shirt, leaving him in just his slacks.

"Wife." It's as if he's testing it out. "Ah. I like it." Theo kisses me more hungrily, and then murmurs, "My wife."

His mouth travels downward, over my wedding dress, all the way to my toes. He brings each one in between his lips, savoring them slowly. "Such sweet, small feet," he says, kissing his way up my calf. He slides up the dress so he can get access to my knees and thighs, and his tail flicks back and forth with anticipation. Hot breath tickles me through my underwear.

"Turn over," he whispers to me, and I hastily obey, wondering what he has planned next. I love when he tells me what to do in bed, because I know I'm going to like it.

His fingers neatly, carefully undo the laces of my dress, and he kisses each new inch of skin he exposes. As he crouches over me, breathing me in, something thick and hard presses at my hip.

"Now sit up." Again I do what he tells me, and he draws the dress up over my arms and head. Then he gingerly hangs it up next to the mirrors, and I wonder if it's so he can look at it while he makes love to me. He sits down behind me, kissing my throat as he lets my hair down.

"You looked amazing in that dress," he says, resting his chin on my shoulder so we can look into the mirrors together. We watch ourselves as his hands roam from my hips up my belly to my breasts, where he tests the heft of each one in his hands. "And you look amazing without it."

"I could say the same about you." I turn my head to kiss his big muzzle. "You were really hot in that tux."

He chuckles as he plays with my nipples. "I love turning

you on. It always smells so sweet." He gets up so he can take off his pants, revealing that sturdy, thick cock I love, and the heavy, dark sac that lies underneath it. Then he crawls onto the bed on his hands and knees, a surprisingly predatory look in his big, soft eyes. He licks his lips as he spreads my legs apart, and gently slides off my lace underwear. He sniffs them, and his ears flatten with pleasure. I've ceased to feel embarrassed by things like this.

He spreads the lips of my pussy wide with his hands, exposing the tender nub hidden there, then leans down to lick. I'm so turned on and sensitive already that it makes me cry out, and he chuckles against me.

"I thought you were tired," he says, and it always pleases me when he gets that mischievous tone in his voice.

"Not anymore," I say between gasps as he continues lapping me with that wide tongue. He nuzzles my clit, then puts two fingers inside me with ease. My body has certainly adjusted to him. "I guess you do that to me, husband."

When I say this word he groans, and hastens the movement of his hand. When I reach my climax it hits me hard, making my back arch high up into the air. He brings his drenched fingers away, using my fluids to wet his own cock.

Usually he likes to get on top of me, where it's easiest to fit, but this time Theo sits down and gestures to his lap once more. "Come here, wife."

The command sends a shiver from my throat down to the hot place at the crux of my thighs. I do as I'm told, his cock now sitting between us. He licks his fingers and then reaches between my legs, making sure I'm soaked for him. Then he lifts me up by the hips as if I weigh nothing, and I grip his cock in my hands as I guide it inside me.

I'm tight at first, my channel swollen up from my orgasm. Theo grunts as I take in more of him. He turns his head to look in the mirror, and nudges me with his nose to do the same.

Instantly, the sight of us makes me clench around him. I can see where his hands grip my hips, his cock gradually vanishing inside me. I can see how my soft belly brushes his big, hard one. He plays with my breasts, then worries my nipples between his thumb and forefinger.

"You're so beautiful, sweetheart," he tells me, kissing my forehead as we take in the sight of ourselves in the mirrors. With his huge hand, he slides me down on his cock even further, and I moan as it sinks in deep. I pull my minotaur close, wrapping my arms tight around his neck. He brushes some stray hair from my face. "You take me so well."

Then we're joined all the way, and I gasp as my clit meets the root of him, rubbing against the soft fur there. I rock back and forth, savoring the feel of him buried all the way inside me and how his fat cockhead teases every sensitive spot I have. Cupping my butt in his hands, Theo lifts me up, and almost slides out of me before he drops me down again. I cry out as it fills me up obscenely, fuller than I could have ever dreamed.

We make love that way, me astride Theo's lap, my breasts bouncing with every stroke and thrust. I kiss his nose, his face, his big muzzle, even his velvety ears. But the longer we go, the bigger his pupils get, until the animal in him has risen high enough to the surface that it takes over.

With a heavy grunt, Theo pulls me off his lap and flattens me down to the bed on my belly, my ass in the air in front of him. He rubs his cock all over my clit, teasing where I want him to be.

"Please," I say, whimpering. "Please, Theo."

When he drives his cock into me, my cry fills the room. Theo fucks me hard now, hard and fast, squeezing my butt as he thrusts in and out in a motion so torturously lovely that it feels like I might collapse. Then he strokes my clit with one hand, his long nose pressed into the back of my neck.

"I'm going to fill you so full," he says low in his throat, so it comes out a rumbling sound. "And then I'm going to do it again."

"Again?" I ask between helpless moans.

"Again."

I can't control what comes out of my mouth as he plunders me thoroughly. All I can do is watch as my ass rocks back and forth in front of him, Theo squeezing my cheeks hard while drives himself in. I'm consumed with the sight of him, the feel of him, and my overwhelming love and affection for him.

"Oh, Theo!" My whole body becomes one single taut string, ready to break at any moment. Theo roars, a sound I've never heard him make before, as my sheath seizes up all around him.

"Fuck, sweetheart." His body curls forward as his own climax takes him over. "You feel absolutely perfect."

He slams into me hard once, twice more, and I feel him swell inside me. When his hot come fills me up, I hit my wave again, and I collapse to the bed with the sheer force of my orgasm. Theo convulses as I drain him dry.

Theo kisses my ear, the back of my neck, my shoulder. "I love you," he whispers, rubbing his nose on my skin. "I love you so much, Celeste."

"I love you, too," I whisper into the comforter.

Then he turns me over, his big cock slipping out of me, and I find he's already stiff and swollen for me again. While I'm still soaking wet and his come is dribbling out of me, Theo crouches over me, his hot breath mussing my hair. He takes my lips in his and, with the tenderest of kisses, he slides into me again.

It is just like I dreamed, where my minotaur takes me all

night in front of those mirrors, loving me with his whole, huge heart.

Epilogue

On the way through the airport, I stay close by Theo's side. There are more monsters here than I've ever seen before, all of them hurriedly walking from one place to another with suitcases in tow. Though many of them stare at me when they realize I'm human, they look away when they see me with Theo.

I've never been on a plane before, so he has to grip my hand tight as we take off. But once we're in the air, Theo introduces me to the marvelous selection of movies. He's seen all of them, so he picks one out for us to watch, and by the end I'm crying into his shoulder. Theo puts an arm around me, tugging me close and kissing my head.

"My wife with the big heart," he says.

After the first flight, we have a layover of a few hours. I feel confident enough to go and get a sandwich by myself, and nothing bad happens except a funny look from a chimera who's also standing in line. When I get back, Theo gives me a radiant smile.

"This is fun," I say, marveling at the planes waiting on the other side of the huge windows. "I always wondered what an airport was like."

"We'll go lots more places, much better than an airport." He kisses my head. "Anywhere you want."

Canada is beautiful, and I watch the steadily-changing landscape out the window of our rented car with awe. The pine trees are familiar to me, but not in this quantity. It's strange as much as it is wonderful.

Theo found us a little cabin on the lake where we would be secluded, with plenty of forest for hiking. The water is freezing cold, but it's fun to splash around for a while anyway. Theo picks me up and dunks me in, making me howl with laughter.

When we're seated in front of the fire that night, snuggled up in a blanket, he squeezes me tight.

"I'm so excited to go on this adventure with you," Theo says, leaning his big head over my shoulder. He rubs his furry muzzle along my cheek, and the tickle of his fur there always makes me giggle. "Just the first of many."

I sigh and lean into him, thinking how I get to spend the rest of my life this way, sitting in Theo's big lap with his arms wrapped around me.

"Thank you," I say, running one hand down his horn to his ear, then over his big cheekbone.

"For what?" he asks, surprised.

"For sending in your application. For choosing me."

Theo squeezes me even tighter. "There was no question in my mind that you were the one," he says. "I knew the moment I saw your photo."

I'm surprised to hear this, given how shy he was when we first met. Heck, how shy he was our first two dates, too.

"You did?" I ask. "But you were so standoffish."

He ducks his head. "I was terrified of making a bad impression. I was so anxious that I'd screw something up and I couldn't stand the idea of scaring you off. I think it got the better of me."

It does make a lot more sense when I think of it this way—that he was paranoid he'd do something wrong so he froze up solid. I feel bad he felt like that, but it only makes me love him even more.

Remembering our first car ride together, I suggest that we put on some music while we enjoy our fireside respite. Theo plays his favorite metal band, who I've come to appreciate because he adores them so much.

We make love there, me sitting astride my huge minotaur husband and swallowing as much of him as will fit, and bouncing up and down on his strong, thick belly. Afterwards, Theo carries me to bed and licks me clean until I'm moaning and ready for him again. This time, he slides in on top of me, sheltering me with his big body. By the time he comes inside me, I'm a shivering, crying mess.

Afterwards we curl up together on the rather small bed, Theo's hooves hanging off the edge. He sighs with pure contentment.

"Where would you like to go next, sweetheart?" he asks, playing with my hair absently.

I have to mull over that. "Maybe somewhere tropical? When it starts to get cold back home?"

Theo nods appreciatively. "I'd like that. I can already taste the piña colada."

After some debate about which countries have the best food, we fall asleep like that, Theo curled around me, my head buried in his soft chest. I don't think I ever imagined I could be as happy as this.

I want someone to spoil.
My minotaur. My husband. My best friend.

～

Thank you for reading!

If you enjoyed this book, please consider leaving a review. Reviews are incredibly helpful to indie authors like me in reaching new readers!

Get the extended epilogue!

Craving even more Theo and Celeste? Head on over to my Patreon to get the two-part extended epilogue!

Patreon.com/LyonneRiley

Join My Newsletter!

For all the latest regarding books, and to get a FREE novella that takes place in the Trollkin Lovers universe, sign up for my newsletter!

www.LyonneRiley.com

For even more stories and lots of NSFW artwork, come check me out on Patreon!

www.Patreon.com/LyonneRiley

About the Author

Lyonne Riley published her first book at age five, which was written on tiny sheets of notebook paper, and she insisted on giving a copy to everyone she knew. She's been writing ever since, from fan fiction in her teen years to original fiction as an adult. After a stint in traditional publishing, she discovered what she truly wanted to write: very smutty stories about monsters and the little humans they worship.

Now she lives in the middle of nowhere with her dogs and spouse, writing sexy fairy tales.

facebook.com/lyonneriley

x.com/lyonneriley

instagram.com/lyonneriley

amazon.com/stores/Lyonne-Riley/author/B0C57K1NM3

Acknowledgments

I would like to thank everyone involved in helping me through the process of putting out this book. I can't say enough how much I appreciate the help and encouragement of the people around me. Thank you to Rowan Woodcock, who created this amazing cover artwork, and Ash Raven for designing it. To my critique partners, Kass, Cia, Ruth and Emily: You all make this possible. And of course, I have to thank my amazing spouse, who has always supported my dreams—and given me lots of inspiration for my characters' sexy adventures.

I couldn't have done this without the expertise of my fellow self-published romance authors. Thank you for inviting me into your circles and helping me through this process.

And thank you to my readers, who gave this book a shot.